Praise for Breaking Even

"A hard-hitting short story collection. Brit Grit at its best."

Paul D Brazill, author of *Guns of Brixton*

"David Siddall understands that sometimes terrible people are wonderful to read about. Siddall's turf is the mean streets of Liverpool, close on a literary map to George V Higgins' Boston or Ted Lewis' Scunthorpe. His subjects are bad luck and trouble. His characters are swindlers and losers who hatch schemes and stab backs. Sharp and bitter and funny, the stories in *Breaking Even* are like car crashes you can't look away from."

Mike Miner, author of *Prodigal Sons*

"An impressive collection of stories, by a talented and versatile author. Siddall's bread and butter is pure Liverpool noir, gritty and atmospheric, breathlessly paced and wickedly funny, but a couple of standout stories set afield prove he's just as good when he broadens his horizons geographically and stylistically both. This guy's a writer to watch."

Owen Laukkenan, author of *The Professionals*

"A full-house of hardboiled crime, followed with six shots, straight into a vein, of pure noir."

Benedict J Jones, author of *Pennies For Charon*

About the Author

A native of Chester, David Siddall is a Liverpool based writer of crime and supernatural fiction. Born in 1963, Siddall left school at sixteen and drifted from job to job until he joined British Rail in 1985. A creative writing class run by the RMT Union under the auspices of Tariq Mahmood – one of the Bradford Twelve – gave him a love of the written word and the encouragement to write fiction of his own. Drawing inspiration from the people and places he has lived and worked, Siddall's novella 'A Man Alone', published by *All Due Respect*, has been described as 'A gripping urban western worthy of a Walter Hill film'. Siddall's stories have appeared in *All Due Respect, Noir Nation, Enoir, Mysterical-e, Albedo One, Supernatural Tales, Beyond the Realm, Fickle Muses* and the anthologies *Our Haunted World* and *Dark Visions 2*.

Breaking Even

David Siddall

And Other Stories

Published by Armley Press 2016

Acknowledgements

Copy Editing: John Lake
Layout: Ian Dobson
Cover photograhy and design: Mick Lake
Production: Mick McCann

The author wishes to thank Mick McCann and John Lake for making this happen; Mick Lake for the superb artwork; and Ann, Marie, Gary and Evie Mae for making life complete. The following stories first appeared in these publications: 'Deadbait' *Noir Nation*, Sep 2013; 'Fake' *All Due Respect*, Mar 2014; 'Part of the Deal' *Enoir*, Sep 2012; 'Sullivan's Steps' *Out of the Gutter*, Winter 2010; 'The Big Shot' *Mysterical-e*, Fall 2008.

For Al, Nige, Sue and Heather. Best friends a man ever had.

ISBN 978-0-9934811-1-6

Contents

Breaking Even   ... 7

Always and Forever   ... 75

Deadbait   ... 100

Fake   ... 124

Part of the Deal   ... 137

Sullivan's Steps   ... 151

The Big Shot   ... 168

Breaking Even

I was never a man to worry about money.

Easy come, easy go was a philosophy adopted at an early age. And not just financially.

Friends came and went with a frequency that bordered on carelessness. Relationships never lasted long. As it turned out, neither did my parents. Dad when I was three, Mum to cancer when I was seventeen.

Obliged to stand on my own two feet, I drifted from one meaningless job to another, and it was there I learnt that what you held in your hand on a Friday night was nothing, just a stake, a gateway to greater riches, putting it all on the grey or the next turn of card. Sometimes it worked and I lived like a king for a fleeting moment of time. More often it didn't, and I scratched around borrowing just enough for bread and milk until the next hit, the next score.

No, I never worried about money.

Not until I didn't have any that is. And when the money I didn't have was owed to a gentleman of a certain persuasion, a persuasion that viewed collateral in terms of broken limbs and severed fingers, then I began to see my disposition in a slightly different light. I was in a bad place, a run of bad luck made for a serious cash flow problem. Problem being it was flowing all one way, and until the tide turned, I was in danger of being swept right out to sea with no way back. Grace had thrown me out, the car was being repossessed, and I was reduced to kipping on a mate's sofa. That, and a guy breathing down my neck for the two thou I'd borrowed and didn't have was making, as the Chinese say, for interesting times.

It was a friend of a friend who told me about Jimmy Wade. Said he might be able to help.

Apart from a few fingers, what did I have to lose?

*

I met Jimmy in the Courtyard. It was a secluded spot shared by Rigby's and The Lady of Mann, the sort of pubs Liverpool was famous for: good beer, unpretentious, and run by people who knew what they were doing. Horse-drawn drays once came through the passageway to unload barrels of ale to the cellars. Now it was paved, lined with hanging baskets, and littered with wooden tables and chairs. In summer it acted as a sun trap, a refuge from the city's bustle. But at any time, it was a good place for men of business to discuss a plan of action. According to the blogs it was Liverpool's best kept secret. Being in the blogs meant it wasn't. Not anymore. But at two o'clock on a grey March afternoon, it wasn't difficult to find a seat.

I was sipping a Fruh, light and malty, its crispness betraying German origins, when he blew in like he had a wasp up his arse. Mobile phone stuck to his ear, he scanned the sparsely populated tables before his eyes settled on me. He nodded to the voice on the phone, held up a finger to acknowledge my presence, and pushed his way through the furniture to where I sat. Throwing himself in the seat opposite, he continued his conversation. Jimmy Wade was younger than me, right side of thirty I'd say, and he had that swagger, the arrogant strut of a man who knew his own worth. Me? I thought he was trying that little bit too hard.

He ended the call, brushed wayward hair out of his eyes, and placed his phone and a fob of keys on the table. He held out his hand. "Daryl, is it? Daryl Chancellor?"

I nodded, took his hand. "Most people call me Chance," I said.

He apologised for being late. I said it was okay but knew he wasn't bothered, it was something to say, breaking the ice before we cut to the chase. Jimmy didn't give a shit whether I was there or not. He was just a go-between, a messenger acting for someone else. A someone I had no interest in knowing or meeting. Less I knew about the man in control, better I felt.

I bought him a beer, thought I should buy into the part of him doing me a favour, and checked my change. Hoped he wouldn't want another. Things really were that bad.

Jimmy sipped, rolled it around his mouth as if mulling over a question before swallowing.

"Looking to make some easy money then?" He smiled, gap-toothed and dishonest but already carrying an air of superiority.

I shrugged, took a drink. Didn't want to appear too keen. "Depends what's on offer."

He chuckled like he knew I didn't have much choice, like he knew I didn't have many options. So he placed his elbows on the table, looked me in the eye, and told me the way it worked.

"Ten grand," he said. "Ten grand, for a week's work." He smiled an "I know something you don't smile" that was already irritating me to hell, and added, "If you could call it work," and winked.

"We fly you to the Caribbean," he held up a hand to stifle a question I hadn't formulated, and continued. "Put you in a five star hotel, and you enjoy a week in the sun courtesy of me and my associates."

Associates my arse. Guy was a prick. He made a mock bow as if I'd won the star prize on a

T.V. quiz. "And?"

"You come back with a little more than when you went. That's all. An item that would be mutually beneficial to all concerned." He smirked. "I mean, you don't get something for nothing in this world."

Drug mule. Won't say I hadn't already guessed. But to hear it spoken aloud? Call it naked fear, but a shiver ran into my pants.

And yet...

I shifted in my seat, lit a cigarette. Ten grand was a lot of money. But then twenty-five years in a flea-bitten West Indian prison with the company of roaches, snakes, and black fellas who saw you as an aperitif to the main course, didn't, on the other hand, hold a lot of appeal. I smiled at Jimmy, told him I'd think about it.

He nodded like he understood. Told me not to leave it long. Plenty of others glad of the opportunity. I watched him go and turned back to my beer. The few coins in my pocket sang like a Greek chorus, pointing out the bleeding obvious. I'd done some dodgy things in the past, but running drugs from the Caribbean? I shook my head. Could it get any worse?

A minute later it did. Ringo Linnick walked into the Courtyard.

Shit.

I thought about the bar and the door to the street. But my back was against the wall, a table in front of me, and Ringo had me in his sights. He sauntered over, walking with a rolling gait that emphasised his bad knees. And if it wasn't poetry in motion, it was an exercise in synchronicity that was a lesson to all.

Ringo wasn't built for speed. They said in his younger days he had been a useful footballer; played for Old Swan or Netherton. Someone said he even had a trial at Tranmere. Then again, who hadn't? But Ringo wasn't the kind of player to go running down the wing or make darting forays into the opposition's box. No. He was more the solid centre-half type. A man marker, the type who played the man rather than the ball; a man who wasn't afraid of hurting his opponent.

His football career held him in good stead for what came after.

Ringo was the go-to guy when people had a problem with late repayments. It was said he kept a little black book with the names of everyone who owed money and the conditions he imposed when taking on the debt for those who employed him. It was rumoured too, that in a separate column, he kept an account of what happened to those who never met those conditions. Now he was acting as the bag man for the guy I owed money to. And the two grand it had been on Monday was now an unhealthy two and a half. And growing every day. Ringo never showed his emotions. But I swear, beneath the grey cropped hair his eyebrows did a little dance as he neared my table.

Ringo placed both hands on the table and stared in my face. Focused, mean, one look conveyed the seriousness of my offence. I tried to stare him out, fumbled in the pack for another cigarette. Ringo knocked them from my hand then crushed the pack in his giant paw. It was the same hand that crushed bones and tore fingers from sockets. The one with adorning rings taken from his victims. I rubbed the onyx ring with the diamond on my left hand, subconsciously placed it beneath the table. It was Dad's. The only thing of value he ever had. And I didn't want it adding to Ringo's collection.

"You got it?"

Typical Ringo. No pleasantries, no "Nice day" or "How you doin', lad?". Always straight down to business. Ringo and I had a love hate relationship. He hated me and I would have loved it if he were run over by a bus. Or hit by a falling piano. I looked skywards. No luck there then. I squirmed in my seat.

"Not exactly."

He cocked an eyebrow. "Not exactly how?"

I made a serious face, opened my hands before I remembered Dad's ring, and quickly placed right over left concealing it from view. "What I mean is, I'll have it soon."

"Yeah?"

"Yeah." And I met his hard eyed gaze with one of my own. "An opportunity has just presented itself," I said and nodded in what I hoped was a confident manner. "Be a good score," and I leaned forward as if this were for his ears only. "If you could give us a few more days, there may be a something extra. For yourself I mean."

Ringo didn't speak or even open his mouth, but I watched his features harden. His brows furrowed like a newly turned field, and his lips clenched that little bit tighter. He grunted, but took his hands off the table. "Not paying now then?"

"Like I said, Ringo. Soon."

"Hope so, Chance. My employer is not a patient man." He pursed his lips as if he were thinking. "End of the week then." He closed once more, pushed his face in mine. "And that'll be three large now." Ringo stepped back, adjusted his jacket. Turning away he took a half step then glanced back. He pointed to my hand. "Nice ring, Chance.".

I didn't reply. Just watched him walk through the passage, out to the street. I had bought a little time. For a few days at least.

That night I checked Wikipedia, hooked into a load of websites, read everything I could.

And the consensus of opinion was, that though the detection of illegal narcotics was so much better than in the past and conviction rates increased, 70% of smuggled goods still went undetected. They were the sort of odds I liked.

I phoned Jimmy, said I'd do it.

*

Three days later I was at Liverpool Airport waiting for the flight to Antigua. So was Julie, my cover. Single guy, week's vacation, alarm bells would be ringing in every custom officer's head. But a young couple, romantic holiday and all that shit? Well, you get the picture. She was a tidy piece too. Dark hair tied in a pony, long legs and a backside so tightly packed in a pair of blue jeans, I wanted to take a bite and say this is mine. My face gave me away. Before I said a word she held up a finger. "Don't get any ideas. This is business. You do your thing, I'll do mine, and we'll get along just fine." She held my eyes a moment longer than necessary then led me through the foyer, security, and into the lounge where she sipped a latte, played with her phone, and pointedly ignored me.

Odds of anything developing between me and Julie? Zilch.

We flew business class. I knew how to act, had put on a jacket and tie. Julie drank champagne, and didn't speak. After collecting her bags she took a taxi and disappeared. I didn't see her until the flight home. Guessed she was an old hand at this.

Outside a private car was waiting and drove me to the Blue Waters Resort. Five star, all inclusive. My employers obviously didn't do things in half measures. I used all the facilities. You never knew. If I got nicked, at least I'd have something to remember. And as the unwilling Julie had found some other avenue of entertainment, I found consolation in the arms of Christa, the hotel receptionist. Maybe she took pity on the absence of a partner, maybe she was looking for a little romance; maybe she was just wanted a good shag. Whatever, any disappointment I had over the wayward Julie dissipated in the ample, 36DD charms, of the lovely Christa.

They came for me at night. Twenty-four hours before the flight home, a message was passed that I should go to the car park at midnight. A bottle-blue sedan was waiting. I sat back, tried to enjoy the ride, but I was sweating like a chimp on heat. My act, playing the cool dude, was fooling no one. Least of all me.

Taken to a clap-board house on the outskirts of English Harbour, I was given four packages.

Four. My heart sank. Each one was the size of a house brick. So much for bringing, an item back. They said to put them in my case and forget they were there. I looked at the guy giving the instructions. Big, black, there were muscles in places I didn't know existed, and a bulge beneath his jacket I guessed wasn't a banana. This, I guessed, was not the time to start renegotiations. Careful not to touch them with my bare hands, I did as I was told then was driven back to the resort. In the morning the hotel staff collected my suitcase and took it to the airport. Weak, but without fingerprints, at least I had plausible deniability.

Julie met me at the airport. Tanned, refreshed, she looked good. Even held my hand through customs.

Nailed it.

Taking off was the best buzz ever. I clenched my fist. Caught now it was a maximum eight in a British nick. Didn't sleep on the plane. My mind was working overtime: how to act, how to react should I be challenged by some jobsworth no-mark wanting to make an impression. I needn't have worried. We collected our cases from the carousel, waltzed through Nothing to Declare and I found myself on the concourse of Liverpool Airport. I closed my eyes, tried to calm my racing heart, and took one huge breath.

And that's when my troubles began.

1

"Daryl, Daryl Chancellor?"

The guy wearing sweat top and pants was looking straight at me. He had greasy hair, bad skin, and an accent so crooked, you could hang a coat on it. Another meat-head, a black guy with a domed head rising above the coral blue of his eyes like an emerging volcanic island, hovered in the background. The foyer was busy. Several planes had landed in a short space of time, and a flood of humanity converged on the exits. Julie had gone. She had boxed off her responsibilities and was already disappearing into the crowd by the door.

The greasy guy came over, tried to take the case from my hand. Inside was a sports holdall with the coke. I moved it to my other hand. "Where's Jimmy?"

He shrugged. "Couldn't make it." He jerked his chin towards the swing doors. "Car is outside."

I hesitated. Plans change, shit happens, and sometimes you have to go with it. But it didn't sit right. I ran my tongue round the inside of my mouth. And it wasn't the plane's air-con that made it taste like ash.

"Come. Please."

I squeezed the handle of my suitcase that bit harder, glanced around the foyer. By the

newspaper stand, a couple of armed cops, airport police, clocked faces, scanned the crowd looking for that one sign, that hint of behaviour that might draw them. I swallowed my nerves and nodded. This wasn't the place to cause a scene. Not with eight kilos of the white stuff in my suitcase. Besides, who but Jimmy knew I was there?

I fell in beside the guy in sweat pants. "What happened to Jimmy?"

He shrugged. "You know. Probably facking some girl or has face in bucket of beer."

I grinned like I knew. Christ, I'd only met the guy twice. But I didn't want these guys to know that. For all they knew I was an old hand at this. I put on a bit of a swagger as we walked to the door.

"George." Greaseball gestured to his buddy to open the door. Passing, I nodded my thanks.

George did nothing except give me a cold fish stare that did nothing to ease my discomfort. He followed as we crossed the car park and hurried to a waiting Mondeo. A fucking Mondeo. Was expecting a Merc or Jag, something with a little class. I glanced at my companions. Maybe these lowlifes were bottom of the feeding chain, hired hands sent to protect the gear, and nothing else. Or maybe a Mondeo didn't stand out from the crowd? Whatever, I was glad of the ride, had started to relax when George opened the boot and waited for me to put the case inside.

"It's okay," I said and our eyes met. His stare was hard, focused, and I tried to match the intensity of his gaze with one of my own. Failed miserably. "I'll keep it with me," I said. "In the back."

There was a glimmer of a smile, like he was amused at my lightweight challenge, but he shrugged like it didn't matter, and closed the boot. I slid the case onto the back seat and followed it in.

The door slammed. Greaseball got in the driver's seat, George beside him. Think it was then

I realised how vulnerable I was. The frig was I doing? A voice in my head was telling me to get out. Take the case and go my own way. I swallowed a ball of saliva. How would it go if I did? Would they try and stop me? Here? I turned my head, looked through the back window. There were people, cops too. I could get out, I should get out. The game was in play. Cash in or let the money ride? Sweat peppered my brow. And then it was too late. Greaseball turned the ignition and the car roared into life. All bets were off. For better or worse, I was along for the duration.

And this was meant to be the easy part.

Still uneasy, I gazed through the window, watched the world pass. It was raining, a miserable drizzle that always seems to fall after a holiday, and says, that's it, fun over. But I wasn't worried about fun, I just wanted to get home in one piece. And my companions were doing nothing to help. Small talk was greeted by one-word answers from the driver, and silence from George. I settled back, closed my eyes, let a sigh escape.

Then my world came apart.

Before we hit the 561 to the city, the driver took a sharp left, and then another on to what was little more than a dirt track. It led to the marsh overlooking the estuary.

Shit, shit, and double shit.

I turned my head one way and then another, gazed out the back window, watched the traffic and street lights fade into the distance. There was nothing out here. Nothing good anyway. The car bounced along the uneven track. "Hey," I said trying to sound confident, hoping this was a bad dream and I might wake up. "What's the score? This isn't..."

I turned back, the words dying in my throat. A semi-automatic pistol was pointed at my head. Saccharine sweet but laced with strychnine, George finally cracked a smile. I began to shake. Felt it working from inside to out. My tough guy act finally ran out of steam. Before I could get a handle on what was happening, the driver turned the wheel right then quickly left, spun the car in the dirt and slammed down hard on the brakes. Like a sock in a tumble dryer, I rolled across the back seat, one way and then another. The door opened, George reached in and put his hand around my ankle. I made a desperate lunge for the suitcase, grabbed the handle just as he pulled. Dragged across the vinyl, my face caught the sill as he yanked me out. Somewhere on the way to the ground, he pistol whipped the side of my head.

I lay in the dirt, stunned, bleeding, and wondering which deity I had upset to have so much go against me. But I was alive. At that moment it wasn't much consolation, but I knew better than to push my luck. I spat out a mixture of mud and blood; shook my head. In my hand was the case. Not for long. A boot slammed my forearm. I screamed and rolled onto my back, clutching my wrist until a foot in the ribs made me double up and retch. Pain and nausea swept through. Beatings I'd taken in the past had been bad, and this was one of the worst. But in the silence that followed, the fear creeping through me was worst of all.

I lay there, listening to the patter of rain, opened my mouth hoping to catch a single drop, and embrace the sensation. For at that moment, I believed it might be my last sensation. Ever. Even that eluded me. I looked up. George was standing over me holding the automatic in a stance straight out of rap school. Acting like he was in some cheap, made-for-TV video, he twisted it from the straight to the side, and back again.

The pain had gone. It was strange, for so had the fear. I'd read somewhere, in the moments before death some take on an otherworldly persona, like they already belonged in a different realm. I closed my eyes, hoped I might see something. But the only realm I belonged in was that of the loser. And I can't say my life flashed before my eyes. If it did, then it wasn't worth the wait. But I will say I was almost serene. I waited for oblivion.

"George."

The word burrowed into my head. I opened my eyes. Pain returned. I groaned and looked to the car. My suitcase was open and lying on the floor, contents spewing forth like a disease. Greaseball was in the driving seat, door open, the holdall with the drugs beside him. "George," he called again, jerked his head indicating the open door. George glanced at the driver then back at me. A second stretched to infinity. Then he took his finger off the trigger, thumbed the safety. I held my breath, watched him climb in the car and slam the door. He stared at me in a way that made me appreciate I was a lucky boy, and it was not his idea to let me live. Then he turned away. I'd been dismissed as someone of little consequence. The car growled into life. I watched until it disappeared into the distance.

I breathed out, winced at my hurt, tried to move. Adrenaline had dulled the pain, now it kicked in with a vengeance. I got to my knees, put a hand out to steady myself, and spewed my guts onto the sodden ground. Dry retching made it worse. Eventually it stopped and I replayed the sequence of events. It didn't get any better. Picked up the dope, nailed the run; then mugged by a couple of wannabes.

Shit.

I stood up, tried to get my bearings. Ahead was the marsh and river, behind the slip road and airport. I knew this place, played here as a kid. Dirt tracks and cycle paths led in all directions. If I kept the lights of the road on my right, I could bypass most of the houses. A couple of hundred yards through the suburbs and I could slip through to the promenade. Apart from the doggers and queers looking to hook up, it'd be deserted. Didn't want to be picked up by the Feds on the main road bloody and shit up. Too many questions. My watch said it was 22:15. It was a four, maybe five mile hike to the flat. Somewhere near the river a curlew's cry split the silence. I took a step, swayed as a stab of pain hit me, and started to walk. It was going to be a long, long night.

2

Banging, banging, bouncing around the walls of my head. I tried to ignore it, wanted to stay in the sweet layer of sleep just that bit longer. It didn't stop. So loud was it, I thought the door might come off its hinges. Rolling over, I groaned as a wave of pain washed through me, and pulled the covers off my head. Still it continued. They were persistent, and loud, and I hoped Spence might answer.

Last night the flat had been empty. Since Grace had changed the locks on the house, and I found my belongings in a bin-bag on the doorstep, I'd been kipping on Spence's sofa. Told him I needed a couple of weeks to sort my head out. Two weeks turned into a month; then two. Not many would do that. Spence was a loner, a night-owl, and kept his own hours. And if I never really knew what was going on in his head, I was grateful for him being there. He was one of the good guys.

I looked across. His bedroom door was closed. There'd be no moving Spence till after midday.

I sat up, swung my legs to the floor. "Okay, okay," I shouted and gave myself a quick once over. There was a bruise running from elbow to wrist on my left arm and a circle of purple on my side. I coughed, felt needles of pain jab through my ribs, wheezed like an old man. Finding a mug with cold tea on the table, I spat.

The small circle of white was flecked with red. Guessed I'd be pissing blood too. Wearing only boxers and T-shirt, I stumbled to the door, released the catch. It was Jimmy. His jaw was set, his face flushed.

"Chance, where the..." His eyes narrowed. "Fuck happened to you?"

My face. I lifted a hand, traced a finger over the place George had struck with the gun. Last night I'd showered, cleaned myself up best I could before falling asleep. But sometime in the night the cut must have reopened. Dry blood caked cheek and temple. Ignoring me, Jimmy pushed past and through to the living room. He threw off his jacket, pushed the duvet I'd been sleeping under to the floor, and bounced on the settee. He was wearing, a stars and stripes sweat: six big white stars over three horizontal red stripes. Looked like a spoilt kid.

"Well?" he said.

"Well what?"

"What happened?"

"Could ask you the same."

"Last night?"

I nodded.

"Flat tyre."

"Convenient."

"Hey it was pissing down and I was up to my arms in shit. When was the last time you changed a wheel in a fucking storm." Jimmy shrugged. "When I got to the airport you were gone."

I grimaced. Saw it for what it was.

"So," he said, what did happen to you?"

"Got jumped by a couple of wannabes."

He whistled. "Where?"

"Outside the airport."

I watched his face change as the first intimation of failure swept through him.

"At the airport?"

"Yeah."

"But you've still got the gear?"

I closed my eyes. "The fuck do you think?"

Finally it filtered through, Jimmy understood. He bounded off the couch. "You having a laugh?" Jimmy was praying, hoping I was. But I dashed his hopes, shook my head. "Shit." He stared at me like I was a freak that had snatched his toys. Jimmy put a hand to his mouth, turned his back, began to pace the floor. He stopped, a lightbulb moment, and came back at me, wagging a finger in my face. "If you're trying it on..."

"Fucking hell, Jimmy," I upturned my arm, held it out, showing the bruise. "D'you think I did this to myself?"

He saw my eyes, saw the truth. Even so. "Been done before, y'know."

"What?"

"People. Think they can get away with it." He shrugged. "Get a couple of mates to work em over, bit of sympathy then enjoy the fruits of their labour." He leaned close. "Eight kilos of the white stuff can buy a lot of Witch Hazel."

"Fuck off, Jimmy."

We eyeballed each other until Jimmy dropped his gaze. He seemed to deflate, sink in on himself as he saw the futility of his reasoning. "Did they leave anything?"

"Just my wallet." I flicked through the compartments. A bit of silver and a few Antiguan notes. I held it out to show him. "That's everything I have in the world."

Jimmy rubbed his chin. "You'll have to see Felix."

Bad as I felt, my stomach flipped. "Felix. Felix McKenzie?"

Jimmy nodded. "It's his stuff you've lost. His gear. He put up the money and you haven't delivered. Sale of goods mate. A contract between supplier and merchant. Goods go missing," he shrugged, "someone has to pay."

Jimmy smirked. He shouldn't have because at that moment all I wanted was to hit him in the mouth. But I held my cool. Didn't need the aggro. Not now. Instead I kept it in, went to the bathroom.

I stared in the mirror. Felix McKenzie. It just kept getting better. Loan-sharking, gambling, importer of narcotics, and every illegality between. I wasn't keen on meeting the great man, especially since, as the way Jimmy put it, I'd managed to lose his precious cargo. But I didn't have much choice. Either I went to him or he came for me. And I knew which way I preferred it. I took a deep breath, reached for my razor. Clean myself up was the first thing. I'd put on a shirt with a collar too. Show I was taking the loss personally. And if things went tits up, I may as well look the best-dressed corpse in the morgue.

Odds of getting out of this one? 2/1 at best.

3

Felix McKenzie was a bantam-weight of a man. He was also a legend. A legend enhanced and enriched in the backstreets of Liverpool. And if that legend relied on events that were a distant memory to those involved, then Felix McKenzie was not one to deny a colourful past. Why have a reputation if it isn't one you can manipulate? He was fifty-two, five-seven, and hard as nails.

Born and brought up in the harsh environment of Belfast's Tiger Bay, a modest boxing career in the 80s got him away from the Troubles. Once that finished, the ruthless streak that earned him success in the ring, brought him, in retirement, the rewards his career hadn't. There wasn't much that went on in Liverpool's criminal underbelly that Felix McKenzie didn't have his fingers in.

We were in his office at the back of Koko's nightclub. He sat at a desk the size of a small car, while Jimmy and I stood like schoolboys before the Headmaster. He was wearing a grape-coloured jacket over a dark, open-necked shirt. Sharp. Very sharp as opposed to the tool that stood at his side. In sweat top and gym shoes, looked like he had just come from pounding a bag. Hoped it wasn't practice for us. McKenzie still had the eyes of a pugilist. Those narrow slits focused on my face as I told him my story.

He didn't say anything, just stared at me. The silence that followed lay like a set of weights across my chest. A moment passed before he flicked his gaze on Jimmy.

"And you?"

"Flat tyre." Even to me it came a little too quick, like Jimmy was waiting for the question.

Again that stony silence. "Convenient."

I stood just that little bit taller and lifted my chin as McKenzie echoed my initial thoughts.

When he turned his gaze back on me, I slumped like he'd unleashed one of his famous right-handers into my gut. Felix McKenzie had that kind of effect on people.

"Tell me again about these wee fellas who's caused me this grief?"

I shrugged, tried to think. "One," I said, "the black fella, was

20

called George." I closed my eyes the better to see his face. But every time I did, all I saw was those cold, blue eyes and that automatic pistol pointed at my head. Still, I tried. "Eh, five-ten, bald..."

"Like me?" McKenzie rubbed a hand over his grey stubble.

"No," I said. "Smooth, shiny like a billiard ball." I glanced at McKenzie.

"And your other man?"

"Foreign guy."

"Foreign?"

"Had an accent. East European. Romanian, Russian maybe." I shrugged. "Something like that."

"And you've never seen them before?"

"Never."

"But you got in a car with them?"

I opened my mouth, stopped myself saying something stupid and swallowed back the words.

"Yes," I said. It crept out.

McKenzie sat back in his chair. "So you land at the airport, walk through customs, are met by two men you've never seen before, and get in their car with eight kilos." He jabbed his thumb in his chest. "My eight kilos of merchandise, the finest grade currently in the city, then let yourself be relieved of it."

I bowed my head, his words lashed me like a steel-tipped whip.

"While you," he said, pointing a finger at Jimmy. "Are sitting at the side of the road changing a fucking tyre." He threw up his hands, looked at his goon. "Fuck are we employing these days?" He leaned forward, elbows on the table, and addressed us both. "Anything about this seems unusual?"

Jimmy and I shared a glance.

McKenzie brought his fist down on the table. "You have a flat and two men you've never met before know you've got a bag full of charlie." He spread his arms wide waiting for one of us to explain. When neither of us answered, Felix took a breath and exhaled slowly, made himself calm down. "Who knew?" He was looking at me.

"No one," I said. "Just me and Jimmy."

"Come on. Girlfriend, brother?" His eyes widened, "Boyfriend? Everyone tells. Human nature, the need to tell someone."

"I swear, no one."

"Mate?"

"Really I..." I stopped dead, felt the flush on my cheeks. Shit.

McKenzie saw every nuance on my face. He had hit the mark and knew it. When he spoke again he was narrow-eyed, sinister, and completely serious. "Now youse listen to me. I had a big investment in that merchandise and I want it back." McKenzie jerked his chin at me. "You opened your gob and said too much, and you," pointing at Jimmy, "should know better when things go tits up. Flat tyre my arse. Some cunt's put a knife in it to be sure." McKenzie paused. "So I'm giving you a chance. Forty-eight hours to get my goods back."

Unsure whether this was a good or bad thing, I nodded sheepishly. Jimmy just stood there, open mouthed, his face paler than the highlights in his hair.

"Well?"

I didn't say anything. The unspoken "Or what?" lingered like a bad smell and with respect to

McKenzie's reputation, seemed fairly obvious.

McKenzie checked his watch. "Time's ticking," he said.

I glanced at Jimmy. He hadn't moved. Grabbed his sleeve, pulled. Still he didn't move, seemed incapable, like he was in a trance trying to understand what "forty-eight hours to get my stuff back" really meant. I tried again. He tottered forward, and placing one foot in front of the other, shuffled to the door behind me.

Outside, Jimmy came out of it. "What'd he mean, forty-eight hours?"

"He means if we don't get the goods back, we're in the shit."

"We? Why we? You was the one lost it."

I started down the stairs. "You think that matters to McKenzie?" I threw it over my shoulder.

Whether he followed or not, I didn't really care.

"Fuck." He stood at the top of the stairs. "Chance. Hey, Chance." He started slowly, one step at a time, then came running. "Where the fuck do we start?"

I walked towards the car and blipped the lock. "To see a man I thought I could trust."

4

I'd known Spence for years, went to school together. Of all the people in the world, Spence was the only one I could call a true friend. And he was the only one I'd let slip the details of the trip to. Just in case. In case I never came back. I couldn't believe he would turn Judas and shop me for a handful of silver. But he was the only one.

In my haste to meet McKenzie, I'd left my key in the flat and the door was locked. Balling a fist, I hammered on the panel: "Spence." Pounded again, tried to raise him from his pit. "It's me."

Jimmy hung back. His eyes darted around the block, anxiously watching the doors until one opened, and a guy in a flowery shirt stuck his head out. "Hey man, what's the noise?"

This wasn't the kind of behaviour one expected in the Baltic Triangle, a gentrified area of converted warehouses and coffee shops where the pretty people played. And the price of an apartment matched that of their ambitions.

I cast the guy a sidelong glance. I'd seen him before, usually when I was pissed and trying to ram the key into the lock in the early hours. Don't think he approved. I wasn't the right sort. "Nothing to worry about bud," I said.

"Well keep the noise down, yeah."

I gave him a full glare, wasn't in the mood. About to tell him to fuck off, I heard something moving behind the door. Instead I cracked a smile, turned back. "C'mon, Spence, open the frigging door."

Paul Spencer was a laid back dude with sleepy eyes and a mouth too full of teeth. He stood in the doorway, hair messed from sleep, wearing a dressing gown over green boxers. A mug of tea was in one hand a slice of toast in the other. His day never started till after twelve.

"Hiya, Chance. Forget your key again?"

I pushed past into the flat. Jimmy followed while Spence closed the door. I waited until he followed me into the living room. "Who did you tell?"

Spence frowned. "Tell? Tell what?" His head swivelled from me to Jimmy and back again.

"C'mon," I said. "You must have said something?"

He shook his head, "Don't know what you're talking..." His frown deepened and he stopped chewing. "What happened to you?"

I fingered the line on my temple. Damned thing was going to scar, just knew it. "That's what

I'm getting at," I said. "The trip". Still he looked vacant. Either Spence was a very good liar or he really didn't know anything. "Antigua," I said.

Light dawned. "Oh right. The 'business trip'. You made it then?"

I just looked at him. "Yeah I made it all right. Did the business, walked through customs, then this happens." I used a finger to circle my face. The cut, the bruises said more than words ever could.

"Ahh."

"Well?"

"Well what?"

"What d'you know about it?"

He screwed up his face. "Fuck should I know anything? Said you were a dick for going.

Fucking hell, Chance, lucky you're back at all."

"Maybe you would have preferred me not to be?"

"At least I'd have me flat back."

I stared at him, looked deep into a face that couldn't hide a lie if it tried. Was the first time he'd said anything about me staying there. Could have said something before. Would have fucked off, slept on a park bench or something.

He looked at the floor. "Sorry, Chance. Didn't mean it like that."

I didn't say anything, but felt my anger slide. Spence had a way of making me feel like a shit. Nothing conscious or sinister, just the way he was. Said it as he saw it. He didn't know anything. That I was sure of. I'd abused his friendship, taken advantage, and let myself drift along on a tide of booze and self-pity for too long. If I got out of this situation I promised to get out of Spence's life, sort myself out. He didn't deserve this shit.

I patted his shoulder, flopped down on the settee, and put both hands to my head.

"That it then?"

I looked up.

Jimmy was wide-eyed, staring. He had followed the conversation, and stood with open arms.

"If Spence says he don't know, that's good enough for me."

"And you're going to take his word?"

"Yep." I put my feet on the coffee table, helped myself to a Rich Tea biscuit from the open packet. I closed my eyes and sighed. A dead end. Yet something was nagging, eating away at the back of my mind. I gazed around the apartment. Finally I had it. The flat was different. Nothing major, but there was a vase with flowers, the bookshelves were tidy, and it smelled – fresh. Even his battered guitar, which had been lying around for years, was hanging from a bracket on the wall. Last night I'd been too preoccupied to pin it down. But now...

Spence sat next to me.

Jimmy watched us, shook his head. "Fuck me," he said. "You may have given up, but I value my balls and want to keep them where they belong."

Spence put down his mug and I offered him a biscuit from the pack. He took one, bit into it.

"Wanna tell me what's going on like?"

I took a deep breath. "Did what I had to, then got mugged by a couple of fuckers. They were waiting for me, knew all about it."

"Shit."

"Shit is right."

Took a moment before Spence understood. His head jerked around to look at me. "And you thought..."

"Sorry mate, but my arse is on the line. Don't get that gear back, then me and my pal," I jerked a thumb at Jimmy, "will be keeping the fishes company somewhere off Perch rock."

"Fuck."

I nodded. Words seemed superfluous.

Spence clapped his lips and frowned. "Still don't see why you thought it was me?"

"You were the only one I told. Wouldn't have except for Grace. If things went tits up, knew

I could rely on you to see things got boxed off. You know, if she sold the house and that."

"Yeah, would have done that. She wouldn't have done a

25

runner with me keeping an eye on things."

"I know that." I clapped his shoulder. "You're a good pal, Spence."

Across the room Jimmy groaned and fell in a chair. It was finished. Even he realised that. I glanced at my watch. Forty-eight hours, or to be precise, forty-seven before Felix and his boys came knocking on the door. But we still had two days. Come on, Chance, think. Options. There were always options. My brain kicked in, started to calculate. I could make a run, lie low for a while. But I had no money and few friends. Outside Liverpool? None at all. And Felix could wait, would still want blood for the insult and hurt to his pride. He was that kind of guy. No. My resolve hardened. It had to be sorted now.

"You sure you never said anything, Spence?" I shrugged. "Accidentally like. Pissed up or something?"

"Course not." Then I watched his face cloud. Spence was quiet. He tugged at his lip as a thought rolled around his head. And then very quietly said, "Only Linnet."

The room fell from under my feet. I glanced at Jimmy, see if I'd heard right. One look at his face said I had. He hadn't moved, was as caught in the moment as I.

"Linnet?" I said.

"Mmm."

"Who the fuck's Linnet?"

Spence looked at me and smiled. It was a faraway smile, a smile of things known only to him. "You wanna see her," he said and closed his eyes, and I swear from the look on his face he was lost in the memory of the last time they fucked. "She's something else, Chance. A real dream."

That was it. The flowers, the smell of the flat; a woman's touch. Since I'd been living there, a few girls had come and gone. Nothing serious, not on their part anyway. But when they went, Spence always fell heavily. Many an evening we spent washing away the sins of our past in the boozers of the city. Comradeship came at the bottom of a glass. Now there was Linnet.

"How long you been seeing her?"

"Week or so." He turned his face, looked at me.

"And you told her about my little trip?"

"What?"

"You told her I was going to Antigua?"

26

His smile faded. "May have mentioned it."

"Fuck me."

"She was interested, Chance."

"Fucking bet she was." Jimmy was up and prowling the floor. He jabbed a finger at Spence.

"So where is this frigging song bird?"

"Ah c'mon. Linnet's not like that. She wouldn't say anything."

"Just like you wouldn't?" Though the words were aimed at Spence, Jimmy was looking at me. He sneered. "Right all along."

I held up a hand, didn't want Jimmy to say anything. Not now. "Where's she from?" I said.

Spence shrugged. "I don't know. Russia, Slovakia, he waved a hand in the air. Romania maybe."

Maybe yes. The guy with the greasy hair and bad skin sprang into my head like a Jack-in-the-box. I made a "Don't say anything" face to Jimmy. Not a word. "And where," I said, "might we find the lovely, talkative Linnet?"

Spence opened his mouth, but words were unnecessary. For at that precise moment, I heard a key turn in the lock, the door open, and the click clack of a woman's heels tapping across the floorboards of the hall. She turned the corner and walked into the living space.

The room seemed to hold its breath.

Linnet was indeed a dream – one of the wet and sticky variety. She halted, gazed at us in turn, then continued to the dining table like she was auditioning for a West End show. Blonde hair, short and stylishly mussed; petite, and red lips – red, red lips rouged to perfection. She flashed a smile.

"Paul, you didn't tell me we were to have guests." Her English was impeccable, her accent, cut like a polished diamond. She placed a white, Louis Vuitton bag on the table and started to unbutton her coat. One button, two buttons, three, and she slipped it off revealing an Isabel Marant leather mini and embroidered lace top that probably cost more than a month's rent. She wasn't wearing a bra. Linnet moved from the table and came to stand by the arm of the settee. Spence rose and kissed her cheek. "Unexpected babe."

I glanced at him. He had a big Joker grin and eyes full of roses. The fuck was he doing with her?

"Well are you going to introduce me?"

Spence seemed to shake himself. "Sure, sure." He held his hand out, guided her like royalty.

"This is my mate, the one I was telling you about. The one who..."

I didn't allow him to finish, stood, and took her hand in mine. It was soft and pale with long delicate fingers. Cold. "Daryl," I said. "Most people call me Chance."

She smiled again. "Mr Chance. Paul's told me so much about you."

I cocked an eyebrow, wondering just how much he had said. Spence looked at the floor.

I returned her smile. "I'm sure he has."

A wisp of hair fell in front of her eyes and as she went to push it away, she moved her head, looked at me from a different angle. "Have we met before, Mr Chance?"

"No," I said. "But I believe I may have run into one of your friends. Last night in fact."

"Oh?"

I rubbed the thin red welt on the side of my face.

Before I could say more, Spence forced a laugh. "Yeah, uncanny really. We were just talking about you."

"Me?"

"Remember me telling you Spence was going to Antigua?"

Linnet frowned.

"Yeah, you do. Said he was going to," Spence theatrically cleared his throat, and lowered his mouth to her ear, "do some business?"

She shook her head.

"You know," he whispered like there was someone listening. "Get some stuff."

Her face lightened. "Drugs. Yes, yes. I remember you telling me now." She slipped her gaze back to me. "Quite an adventure."

Was there a note of admiration in her voice? Maybe. And even though she was number one suspect for the nark who had given us away, I couldn't help puff out my chest, and stand that little bit taller. Linnet had a way of making you feel honoured she had noticed you.

"Fuck this." Jimmy had heard enough. He bounced up from his chair. "Ask her what she knows will yer?"

28

Linnet's eyes narrowed. "And you are?"

"Oh yeah," Spence stammered. "This is..."

"Doesn't matter who I am. Just ask her."

"Don't think I like you."

"Like I care. What I do care about is still having my cojones at the end of the week."

"Jimmy," I held up a warning finger. "I can handle this."

"Like you're handling it now?" He barked a laugh and made a show of looking at his watch.

He tapped the face. "Time, Chance. There's only so much of it. Ask her who's she working for?"

Linnet's puzzled face switched from Jimmy to Spence and then to me. "Working for? I don't understand."

"Look," I said, "it's like this..."

Jimmy shook his head. "Maybe we should just fill the bath with cold water."

I stared at him. "And?"

"You know. Do what they do." He made a motion of holding someone's head under water.

Spence's face darkened. "Hey."

"Hey what?"

"That's my girlfriend."

"Yeah? And that's the tart who's sold us out."

"Guys." I held up my hands, placed one on Spence's chest as he started across the room towards Jimmy. There was a pause as I waited for the testosterone levels to drop, and for Spence to take a step back. Spence wasn't a fighter. But there are times when a man has to step up to the plate. The fire in his eyes dulled as he shrugged away my hand. The tension eased. But it could kick off anytime. Had to keep an eye on the boys. I made a placating gesture. "If Linnet knows anything, I'm sure she'll tell us," I said and lightly touched her wrist. "Won't you?" My heart was racing but I tried my most engaging smile.

She stared blankly at me.

"It's like this," I said. "Only Jimmy and Spence knew about the trip and when I would be arriving back in England. And then Spence told you. Some people were waiting for me, people who shouldn't have been there, people who shouldn't have known anything about it. Bad people Linnet. You follow?"

"And you think..."

29

I held up a hand. "Maybe you just mentioned it to one of your mates? Over a drink perhaps, having a laugh like?"

"No, no. I only say to my cousin."

A light flipped on in my head. "Your cousin?" A window of opportunity opened.

"Yes."

"And who is your cousin?"

Linnet pursed her lips as if she were thinking whether it was wise to tell us. Eventually she said, "Alexander. Alexander Skrble."

The hairs on the back of my neck stood on end. I glanced at Jimmy. He was whiter than the stars on his jumper. I tried to speak but a cold hand gripped my throat, squeezing the life out of me until I could hardly breathe. I cleared my throat. "Did you say..."

"Screwball." Jimmy was shaking his head. "Your cousin's Screwball?"

Linnet nodded.

I closed my eyes. That window of opportunity just had a brick thrown right through the middle. "Shit."

"Yeah," said Jimmy. "Very big shit."

5

Alexander Skrble was a thug, a "playa" in the games gangsters played, and a man I wasn't keen to meet at all. He was Slovakian, Czech, something or other East European, and his name so indecipherable that in typical scouse parlance, he became known as Screwball. It fitted. His reputation was one of violent unpredictability.

And this was the guy who had Felix McKenzie's merchandise.

According to Jimmy, Screwball had a base in a back street pub called Bennett's. Boozer downstairs, pool hall on the first floor. Jimmy said it was where he conducted his business.

It wasn't hard to find. Jimmy sat next to me as I drove, saying nothing and chewing his nails.

Guess he had a lot on his mind. I pulled in at the kerb and stared through the windscreen. Place was a dive. If someone said it had been condemned, I wouldn't have argued the point. Tried looking through a couple of ground floor windows. They were dirty, wire-meshed, indistinct shapes, and a flashing games machine was all I could see. Upstairs, the yellow glow of artificial light perforated slatted blinds. I strained my neck, wanted to get some idea of what I was getting into. Hoped Screwball was there. At the same time, hoped he wasn't.

I closed my eyes, held a breath. The turmoil in my guts had yet to still. I blew the air out of my mouth – all the way until I could feel lung against chest, then sucked air through my nose, and held it again. Some years ago, I'd been stopped in the street by a Buddhist monk asking for donations. I gave him a couple of quid, he gave me a book: Inner Calm – Fifty techniques to improve your life. Meditative breathing was number one. It was the only thing I read. But right now a Tibetan monastery halfway up a mountain seemed pretty appealing.

I opened my eyes.

"What're we gonna do?"

I let the breath go. "Tell him."

"Tell him what?"

"That the merchandise was for Felix and he wants it back."

"And?"

I shrugged. "Felix is a big name. Bigger than Screwball, right?"

"Well, yeah."

"So I tell him if he gives it back that will be the end of it. If it isn't handed over..." I opened my arms, made a face, and realised I was acting like some bit part actor in The Godfather. Made myself remember who I was. Hoped Jimmy hadn't seen.

"That it?"

I looked at Jimmy, nodded. "That's it."

"You think Screwball's going to say, sorry, here you go?"

"Yeah."

"He's a fucking nutter, Chance. You're liable to get your head kicked in."

The thought had occurred. But so had the idea that Screwball was all front, his reputation doing much to cower those lower down the ladder. If so, Felix McKenzie's name would slash the odds in my favour. "You got a better idea?"

Jimmy said nothing, just stared through the windscreen.

"Thought not." I cracked the door, paused with one leg out.

"You coming?"

Jimmy turned his head, looked at me as if I'd asked him to stand in at my hanging. "Am I fucking shite."

"That's what I thought." I got out and slammed the door.

I was right, Bennett's was a dump. A gateless opening in a wall led to a barrel-stacked yard, and a fire door propped open with an empty beer crate. Metal stairs ran up to the first floor. It was worse on the inside. Cramped, squalid, there was an odour of men and stale beer creeping around the legs of the tables where a skeleton crew of drinkers with yellow-tipped fingers and hacking coughs wasted an afternoon on Aussie white and the Racing Post. But then Bennett's was warmer and cheaper than being at home.

The bar ran down the terminally ill left side and ended at the stairs. I bought a beer from a woman who looked as worn as the counter, and began to climb to the first floor. It was too early for booze, but I sipped anyway, wincing at the metallic taste. I guessed the beer was as out of date as the place.

At the top, carpeted in anaemic red, a corridor led to a pair of swing doors. I pushed, quickly scanned the large room. Nine pool tables in sets of three, low ceiling with spotlights, bar stools lining the walls. It was tidy, looked after, felt like someone cared. Five tables had games taking place. Some laughter and subdued talking filtered from the players. At the far end, overlooking the yard, a table was set apart from the rest. A couple of lads lounged against the fire escape, blew cigarette smoke out of an open window, and watched the game. Chalking his cue was the greaseball I'd met the previous evening. On a bar stool overlooking the room, his partner George. And crouched over the table making his shot was a man I'd never met but heard so much about. Alexander Skrble.

Heart sank into boots. The fuck was I doing? Knees, already weak from thinking too much, buckled. I reached out, gripped the door to steady myself, and hoped no one saw. George had. Some sixth sense, inherent in men of his kind, whispered my presence. Those blue eyes fixed me like a reptile does an insect, pinning me to the spot. Without moving his head, he said something to Screwball.

Over the table and lining up his shot, Screwball paused, then cued the white hard into a yellow. It sank into a corner pocket. He stood over the table, replayed the shot in his mind. Satisfied, he looked at me. And that's when I saw him, really saw him. Black hair shaved at the sides, carefully cultivated stubble to keep that three-day look, and hard, hard eyes. His wrists were surprisingly thin, and his hands had long, delicate fingers. Mum would have called them artist's hands. But then Mum said a lot of things. A shark's tooth, mounted in gold, hung from a chain around his neck. He eyed me for a few seconds then turned back to the table.

He didn't look much, a man you might find fixing the plumbing or pointing a wall. A regular guy. But Screwball had a reputation. A bad one. And whether that reputation was true, false or the make believe of those who felt the need to hear their own voices, who was going to challenge it? You never knew. It just might be true?

And I was going to test that reputation. I took a couple of shallow breaths, stilled the nausea in my belly, and crossed the room. Trying to look the part, I put on a bit of swagger. I'd done some crazy things before but this... Yet walk I did. Strange thing was, with every step my confidence grew. Heart rate dropped, perspiration slackened, I was in the zone. An aura of invincibility I had no right to expect cloaked me. Halting a few feet from the table, I clasped my hands. No threat, just determined. A man here to do business. From the corner of my eye I saw George move his right hand a little closer to his waistband.

Screwball took his shot and another yellow slipped into a side pocket. He hit it with a lot of bottom and the white spun back to leave an easy shot to the top left-hand corner. Again that satisfied smirk. He raised himself from the table and before I could say anything, waved a hand. "Hello." A moment later his attention was back on the table.

I was expecting confrontation, anger, all of those things, and had rehearsed my lines a thousand times, gone over every possible reaction, and worked out a counter. Screwball's action threw me off. Was it something he cultivated? Or maybe we were all wrong and he really was a friendly guy.

Maybe.

I cleared my throat.

He looked at me again, squinted, moved his head side to side trying to decide whether he should make the effort and speak. "Who're you?"

"Is the guy – " Greaseball started to speak but Screwball raised a hand, stopped him.

"Daryl Chancellor," I said. "Chance to most people."

"Should I know you, Chance?"

"No." I put on my smoothest smile and cast a sidelong glance at George. "But I've met some of your friends."

"Yes?"

"Yes," I said.

"Then you must have run into my good friends Pesca and George."

I made a point of touching the wound on my face. "Run into," I said, "is probably the right description."

Screwball looked at me, made a so-so face then went back to his game. He closed one eye, lined up his next shot. "So, is there something I can do for you, Daryl Chancellor?"

"Mr Skrit...." I had practised long and hard. Didn't want to make a mistake and insult the man. But my mouth felt like it was full of sand. I tried again. Mr Skrit...

Faintly amused, Screwball took his shot. Played it soft, off the cush and into a side pocket. There was a murmur of approval from the boys by the fire escape. Screwball was already lining up his next shot.

I hesitated. I was going to ask this man to hand over eight kilos of charlie to the guy he had taken it off the day before. At that point I saw the ridiculousness of the situation. Why should he? All I had to bargain with was Felix McKenzie's name. But what else could I do? It was gambler's choice. And I was never one to shirk a bet.

I coughed, made him look at me, then just came straight out and said it. "I believe you have something of mine. Something that was taken from me in a manner that caused me," I took a breath, "and my employer some distress." I had thought long and hard about what to say. Maybe my words were a little formal, but I reasoned, it got the message across.

Silence encased the table. Inwardly I smiled. My words seemed to have had the desired effect. My bubble burst as the boys lounging against the fire escape doubled up laughing. Pesca smiled. George cast me a stony glare. I didn't move. Didn't dare. My scalp itched and my skin crawled. But I didn't move.

Screwball peered at me beneath knitted brows. He

scratched his chin, seemed to examine me, weighing up the sort of man that would confront him in his own back yard. Crazy? Foolish? Or something else? Satisfied, he leaned back over the table and fired another yellow into a pocket. Only three were left.

"Your employer?" he said, and rose from the table. Any amusement drifting around the table was gone. Now it was just deadly silence.

A flutter of excitement tickled my belly. Hooked him. I forced myself to breathe easy, put on a smile that said I was a man of substance and not without back-up. "Of course," I said. "You don't think this was a private venture?"

He nodded, saw the logic. "Do you play pool, Mr Chance?"

"Sorry?"

"Do you play?" He used the cue to gesture at the table.

I hesitated. I could, even won a few bob in the past playing the soft lad and taking others for a ride. But I wouldn't jump in a pool with sharks; and I wouldn't play a shark at pool. So I kept it cool. "Poorly I'm afraid."

He smiled. "As you see, I play. And when I play, I like to win." Without much thought he cued another yellow into a pocket. Two left. He moved around the table. Down on his haunches, Screwball squinted along the line for his next shot. Satisfied he went back and bent over the table.

"Most times, it is only the winning that counts. The game," he raised an arm and gestured to show his ambivalence, "is nothing." He potted a long yellow and moved to his final ball. It was wedged behind two reds and would take a miracle to sink it.

"You see," He patted his chest. "I come here with nothing, but I work hard to make something of myself." Screwball made an exaggerated shrug. "If it went tomorrow, I say, so what?" He stopped, looked into my eyes, and I saw what so many others had seen in the past; a darkness that lingered on the edge of sanity, and I realised what a mistake I had made coming here to confront this man. For many, it was the last thing they had ever seen.

And then he smiled. It was dark and spoke of things you wished you never knew. He waited, let me absorb his menace before wagging a finger in my face. "But you should know, Daryl Chancellor. Once I have something," he bent over the table, "I never let go." He thrust the cue hard into the white, cannoned it off the cush and doubled the yellow into the right side pocket. It was masterful, genius – and he knew it.

He turned his face on me and I saw the utter futility of my quest. This man had no fear, no respect for anything other than himself, and there was nothing I could do.

But there was this voice inside me. The same voice that said the nag can't lose, the one that said put on a ton, not just twenty; the one that said put it all on red. Screwball lowered himself over the table and gently pushed the white into the black. It was an easy shot and I watched it roll slowly towards the top right pocket. Just before it disappeared, I put my hand out and covered the hole. It was an instinctive act. The ball rebounded off my knuckles and rolled back across the table. No one moved. It was like a single frame left on a movie screen. Just before the celluloid sprang into flame. Screwball raised his eyes, met mine.

It was now or never. I placed my fists on the table, lowered myself to Screwball's level and went eyeball to eyeball. It was my only move, and I played my only card. "Felix McKenzie wants his goods back. And if you don't give it to me, he'll come and get it himself."

The silence dragged on.

Screwball moved first. He rose from his prone position, scratched the side of his head, looked me up and down. Then he turned and looked again at the table. At the black that sat amongst the reds, and at Pesca who would surely now win the game. Pesca never moved but his heavy eyelids had opened almost halfway. George sat there. Waiting. No expression, his features blank.

Screwball stared at the floor, then at his cue. "Felix McKenzie," he said and nodded.

Then so quietly that I barely heard, repeated, "Fe-lix Mc-Ken-zie." Each syllable stretched like he tasted it, rolling it around his palate, wondering if he should spit or swallow. He lifted his head, met my eyes with a fourteen-carat stare, and the blood froze in my veins.

"You come to me and shout," he pushed out his bottom lip and mimicked a child's whining voice, "Felix McKenzie."

He walked around the table, looked me up and down. My feet wouldn't move, felt like they were cased in concrete. Couldn't even take a step back. So I did the only thing I could, held up my head, puffed out my chest.

"You think I care about Felix McKenzie?" he said and stared at me like I was something stuck to the bottom of his shoe. I opened my mouth, thought to bull it out, and that's when he hit me with the cue. It was so quick I hardly had time to realise what was happening. Changing stance and spinning the cue, he used a two handed grip to swing the thick, heavy part at my head. The crack resonated through my brain. Lights flashed; then darkness. Overwhelming darkness that pulled me down, and kept pulling. Tried to keep my feet but it was no use. Gravity won. I crashed hard.

Somewhere outside the zone, I heard a babble of voices, laughter. Someone said, "Good one La". But I was past caring. And still his voice. "Piece of shit. McKenzie shit. You shit." A glob of phlegm splattered my face. I could do nothing, didn't have the energy to wipe it away. "You tell Mckenzie. He want it, he come get it."

His voice moved further away. "Take out the garbage."

There was a scuffle of sound before hands grabbed my arms and legs. My head swam, thought I was going to puke. A door opened. Air. Had to be the fire escape. Half carried, half rolled down the metal stairs, I remember hitting the concrete surface of the yard. Dragged, then pushed against a wall, they had thrown another couple of punches and left me in a heap. It took moments, painful moments of semi-consciousness, to realise they had gone. A cold wind skirled around the yard. I felt bare, torn apart, my naivety exposed to the world. Did I really think I could have got away with it? Did I really think I could walk into Screwball's domain, take back what was mine? I tried to move, rolled onto my stomach.

And I wasn't as alone as I thought.

George was leaning against the wall, grinning, mocking me for the fool I was. Moving with deliberate ease, he lifted a leg, placed his foot on the back of my neck, pushed me into the ground. Slowly he increased the pressure. Face down, I began to choke. Could do nothing and George knew it. I flapped like a fish. On the point of passing out, the pressure eased and he removed his foot.

I took a breath, coughed out some shit and rolled on my back. George watched then raised his foot again. I braced myself, knew he could snap my neck if he wanted.

"Wait," I said and held up a hand. "Why are you doing this?"

Foot inches above my face, George was making a point the only way he knew. "Because I can." His voice was silky, smooth like a mouthful of dark chocolate. "You have to learn," he said. "And anyway." George's smile creased his black face like a knife slash. "I enjoy it." He took his foot from my face, paused, then dug me in the ribs with the toe of his boot. It was the ultimate power trip. Letting me know he could destroy me whenever he wished. I twisted away, waited for what was to come. But for George, it was enough. He had made his point. Turning his back, he headed back to the warmth of his companions. The guy was a psychopath and I was lucky to be still breathing.

Eventually the world stopped spinning. Everything hurt: back, legs, flesh was raw from the metal steps. I moved my head. Felt like some of it was missing. Marching into Screwball's HQ like I'd just done, maybe it'd been missing a while. I wanted to stay and lick my wounds, but the sooner I was away, the better. Took a breath, started to move. Shoes. A pair of brown leather brogues were pushed under my nose. Expensive. Italian. Ringo Linnick. The day wasn't getting any better.

Ringo squatted down so he could look in my face. He shook his head. "Well, Chance, you don't look so good."

"Yeah? Well you wanna see the other fella."

"Eh?"

I hung there, on all fours as if I were about to do fifty push-ups. I grunted. "Nothing," I said and waited for the next episode in our personal melodrama. Nothing came. When at last I moved my head and looked at him, Ringo was staring like he was trying to work something out. Eventually the cogs in his brain stopped turning.

"I guess you got what was coming," he said. "Nothing I can do to add to that."

"Thanks."

"Here," he said, and handed me a linen handkerchief. I rolled over, sat with my back against the wall. "And I wouldn't go thanking me. Not yet."

I wiped my nose and rubbed my head. Blood, almost black, stained the cloth.

Ringo said nothing but watched every move.

I started to rise but Ringo put out a hand, placed it on my head. "Don't think this gets you off the hook, Chance. You've got yourself in some deep shit. But that don't matter to me."

"Thought not."

"You still owe. This is just a temporary stay and the sooner you pay your debts, the better for everyone." He jerked his chin at me to emphasize his words. "Do what you have to do, and you'll find everything falls into place."

"You're all heart," I said.

"Hey." Like a cloud passing the sun, his face darkened. "I'm giving you a chance, Chance."

Ringo waited, see if I caught the humour, but I just wanted him to piss off so I could curl myself in a ball and go to sleep. He sighed, started to rise. "Word of advice. When you front someone like Screwball, make sure you have an advantage. Something they don't expect. Take them out of their comfort zone." He looked down at me, see if his words registered. "This," he lifted a finger and used it to circle the air, "was fucking stupid."

Thanks, Ringo. Think I figured that out for myself. He started to walk, stopped and looked back. "You can keep the hanky, Chance."

I watched him move through the debris of the yard with that rolling gait that reminded me of a ship riding its anchor. He left me in the yard, nursing my head and thinking on what he said. And that's where Jimmy found me. He pulled me up, guided me to the car, and bundled me into the back seat. At last I could close my eyes.

Two hidings in two days. My luck stank.

*

Jimmy drove to Spence's flat, helped me up the stairs then dumped me on the settee. I closed my eyes not knowing or caring what was going on. A cold water compress was pushed on my head and a towel covered my eyes. There were words, harsh words, and heavy footsteps, as the guys paced back and forth wondering what to do. Spence was pensive and worried about me. Jimmy was frantic, worried about himself. At one point his anger bubbled over and he shouted in my ear, "What the fuck did you think would happen you soft get?" I ignored him and lay there, taking it all, giving nothing back. I was too exhausted.

After what seemed an age, their frustration broke. Quiet words followed: "You okay, Chance? Chance. You listening?" And words said to each other.

"You reckon he'll be all right?"

"Dunno. D'you?"

And then I slept.

I drifted in and out. An hour, maybe two of grateful oblivion passed before I opened my eyes and stared at the ceiling. The apartment was silent. I followed a dust mote on its downward spiral, took a few shallow breaths. Someone was there, watching. I raised my head. Hammer blow throbs bounded around my skull. I groaned, loudly, looked over the back of the settee. Linnet was sitting at the table, cigarette poised in her delicate fingers. She said nothing, but her pale face regarded me with an interest I found flattering and unnerving at the same time. I shivered. There was something in her eyes that reminded me of her cousin. The way Screwball looked just before he brought his pool cue crashing against my head.

It wasn't something I wanted to be reminded of.

"Hi," I said

She bobbed her head. "Hi."

A wave of pain swept through me. I winced, screwed up my eyes.

"Pain, yes?"

"Yes," I said. "Pain." I took a deep breath. "It'll pass." I scanned the room. "Where're the boys?"

She shrugged. "Out."

Whatever Spence saw in her, and there was plenty to see, it wasn't for her for sparkling conversation. I hoped she could cook. "Did they say where?"

Same shrug. "Just out." She took another drag of her cigarette, stubbed it out in a saucer, and wafted the smoke away. With what seemed an effort, she rose from her chair and came to where I was sitting. She handed me a glass of water and pushed two paracetamol into my hand.

I looked at the white pills. "What's this?"

"Paul said I should give them to you. For the pain."

I raised an eyebrow. It was a small kindness, but the first in a while. At least I had Spence on my side. They stuck in my throat almost as much as the mess I was in. Washed them down with the water.

"Better?"

I grimaced. "Getting there."

Linnet smiled, showed me her perfect white teeth, and lifted my feet so she could slide onto the couch beside me. My legs she placed across her lap. "The meeting," she said, "with my cousin. It did not go well?"

Conscious of her nearness and the softness of her thighs, I turned my head to the side, showed her the twin red marks either side of my temple and rubbed the freshest. I stopped myself saying something stupid and nodded. "No," I said. "It didn't."

Linnet cocked her head and half smiled. "My cousin," she said, "can be a pig."

My anger flashed. "Yeah. A fucking animal is right." There was a moment as our eyes met of complete understanding. A shared experience perhaps? Something in her past? Who knew what had gone on in her father's barn or under a fucking hay cart? We held each other's gaze a moment longer than felt right, then laughed it away. I was hurting, but still laughed. There was something in her manner that washed me clean, made me forget what had gone before. It was that feeling you get after the tide has turned and you walk a strip of virgin sand looking for what the sea has brought in. And I had always been a curious guy. I was curious about this girl too, this very desirable girl sitting close, and I mean in very close proximity. Close enough for her smell – cinder, burnt orange, and a touch of cinnamon – to catch the back of my throat. Something other than curiosity stirred within me.

Linnet dropped her gaze while I pulled myself together and for something to do with my hands, touched what I imagined was a blue and purple streak at the side of my head.

Her eyes creased. "It hurts?"

"Only when I think too much."

"Uh?"

"Yes," I said. "It hurts." She reached long fingers to my face and I shied away, turned my head until she clucked her tongue, comforted me with words in a language that meant nothing, and I felt like a child beneath a mother's touch. Her fingers were ice; soothing, caressing, she massaged my temples making small circular motions with her fingers. I sank into the pillows beneath my head.

"You like?"

"You've got good hands."

"People say this before."

"And I'm sure they'll say it again." As she followed me forwards, my eyes were drawn to her her small breasts jiggling like they needed to break free of her top. What could I do but help?

Christmas had come early. And it put a smile on my face.

She was right over me now, her scent stronger, both hands working the sides of my head. I breathed deep. Beneath the perfume an intense, animal musk seeped from her pores, sank into my senses, and brought out my basest desires. I swear Linnet purred. She had moved her legs, straggling me like a cat does a plaything. Christ. And still her hands moved, round and round, up and down, and I realised I wasn't as hurt as I thought.

"These drugs," she said. "They are worth much?"

"Fortune," I said and rubbed my thumbs over her nipples. They were hard and standing to attention like soldiers on parade.

"How much?"

She was making me think when I didn't want to.

"I don't know. Quarter of a mill maybe. More when it's cut."

Just for a moment her fingers stopped moving. It was no more than a stutter before she started again. "What are you going to do?" I raised my brows and grinned. She saw, playfully slapped my cheek, and quickly added. "About my cousin?"

Taking my hands from her breasts I placed them on her hips and pulled her towards me. "At this moment, it doesn't seem that much of a problem."

We stared at each other. Her big eyes shone with something I couldn't quite fathom. Maybe it was satisfaction I had acted in the way expected. But the truth was I didn't care. Her skirt had ridden over her thighs and she looked at me like my hands were on fire. She came closer, brushed my lips with her own then squatted on my groin. Linnet ground into me. Just like her hands, round and round, back and forth. My hardness pushed through her panties. She reached down, started on my zip and...

I heard the key in the lock.

When Spence and Jimmy came in, I was lying with my back

to the room. Linnet was sitting in the armchair, clothes adjusted, a glossy magazine on her lap.

We were quiet, perhaps too quiet, for Spence's footsteps stopped just inside the doorway.

"What's going on?"

I waited until he moved to the centre of the room then turned my body so I was facing where he stood. I pinched the bridge of my nose, groaned as if I'd just woken. "Mmm?" The threat of discovery had reduced my libido to normality. Spence's face, questioning and confused, looked from me to Linnet. She tried to look innocent. Difficult when her rumpled skirt showed more than the designer intended. When Spence looked away she used a hand to smooth the creases.

If Jimmy felt the tension, he didn't say. "You awake, soft arse?" He pushed away my legs, bounced down on the couch, passed me a can of lager. He threw one to Spence then put the bag on the coffee table. Looked like we were in for a session. Spence had a face like a child who's seen his favourite toy passed to another. He played with the ring-pull, thought for a second, passed the tin to Linnet. Got himself another, and watched me beneath the deepest frown I'd ever seen. I didn't look. Just cracked the tin and drank. Drank again. Hadn't realised how thirsty I was.

No one spoke.

Jimmy put his can down and started rolling a spliff. He gave me a sidelong glance and shook his head. "So much for the great plan then." He made a show of checking his watch. "Suppose I'd better start thinking where I'm fucking off to."

"How d'you mean?" said Spence.

"Well I aint going to hang around here waiting for Felix and his crew to turn up with a pair of bolt-cutters and surgical tape." He checked the quality of his spliff, licked the edge and rolled it between his fingers. "I mean, what the fuck was the point?"

"Point?" I said.

He paused before placing it between his lips. "That fucking lark with Screwball. You get a hiding, and we're still no closer to getting the gear back." He struck a light.

I glanced around the room. Linnet sipped delicately from the can, Spence had a face like a smacked arse, and Jimmy, enjoying the first wave of hemp, was temporarily lifted from the rock bottom place he'd been a moment before. I brought the can to my lips, finished what was left. My head throbbed and my body ached, but something inside stirred. It was the kind of buzz I got when an outsider was coming up on the rails. "We know one thing," I said.

"Yeah?" Jimmy turned his head. "That we're fucking screwed?"

I ignored him. "We know Screwball really does have the stuff."

"What?"

"Before it was speculation. Now we know it for real."

"Knowing and doing something about it are two different things."

I felt myself frown. Sad to say, it was the truth. I tossed the empty can on the table, reached for another. Ringo's words came back to me. "What we need is an edge," I said, and rubbed my chin. "Something unexpected."

Jimmy shook his head and went back to his spliff. Spence was tapping his nails against his tinny. Wasn't even sure he was listening. And Linnet – Linnet was watching me like the cat that caught the canary. What came next just sort of slipped out.

"What we need," I said, "is a gun."

There was a moment of absolute silence. Spence looked at Jimmy wondering if he'd heard right. Jimmy barked a laugh. "You completely bonkers? Ha. A fucking gun. Do you know how to use one? D'you know where to get one?" He shook his head. "Completely fucking bonkers." He stubbed out his spliff and went for another can of lager.

I sighed. Jimmy was right. It was absolute madness. But the more I thought, the more convinced I became that it was the only way. True, I knew fuck all about guns, but... My heart began thumping.

Linnet sipped from her can. She had drawn her legs beneath her and, if anything, her features had softened, relaxed to a point of satisfaction. I caught her eye, knew she had something to say. She didn't let me down.

"I can get you a gun," she said.

6

Linnet said she needed twenty-four hours. She didn't ask for anything. Not a penny. This of course, was a good thing. I told her to do it, said I'd meet her in the Courtyard at midday. Time was up. Could she actually put her hands on a shooter like she said?

I let out a long sigh, tried to get a handle on my feelings. Guns, gangsters, and a leggy blonde with more balls than Sepp Blater at a World Cup draw. Ran a hand through my hair. So much for playing the big man. The fuck was I doing? Even if she could get a gun, could I use it, actually point it at someone? Last night I found sleep impossible, gone over every possibility, every variation. And with less than twenty four hours to Felix McKenzie's deadline, I had convinced myself that every outcome was a bad one.

I sipped my beer. It had rained. Grey puddles dotted the yard. The hanging baskets looked bedraggled, water dripped from the gutters. The scene matched my mood.

And then she came.

The stubs from half a pack of cigarettes lay in the ashtray, and I had just sparked up again when Linnet came in off the street. She was wearing a short, black jacket that extended to her thighs, barely covering the skirt beneath. I did a double take. For a second it looked like there was nothing beneath the jacket. I swallowed, watched her move with easy grace. She came straight over, kissed my cheek. As she sat, her leg brushed mine then nestled against my thigh. Felt like a bolt of electricity.

By this time a few others had drifted in. For the most part they were office workers, smokers, here for a liquid lunch and a fix of nicotine. A low hum of conversation competed with the output from the kitchen's air-con.

"You came."

"Of course." And of all the variations that had flown around my head, the one where Linnet never showed, had not occurred.

Reluctantly I moved my leg. "Drink?"

She nodded and I went to the bar, ordered a glass of beer that originated in the Czech

Republic. Thought it might make her feel homely. When I returned she had helped herself to a cigarette and was hauling the nicotine into her lungs like her life depended on it. She saw my look and held up the cigarette. "Paul," she said. "He does not like it."

I passed her the beer and sat, my leg finding hers like a magnet. "He's like that," I said.

"Doesn't approve of the weed." I raised an eyebrow. "On the other hand," I said remembering Jimmy's spliff, "there's certain other weeds he has no objection to."

She laughed and brought her bag to the table. It was the same white Louis Vuitton from the day before. I swallowed, raised my eyes to hers. "D'you have it?"

"Oh yes." She started to open the bag before I moved a hand and closed it around hers. I dipped my chin, indicated it would be more discreet if she were to place the bag beneath the table. A grunt of understanding, a crooked smile as if I were a fool to worry over such things, and she lifted the bag from the table, placed it on her knees and unclasped the fastener. Prising it open, she reached in and withdrew an object wrapped in a white linen cloth. Placed it on my lap. Shit. A coldness that had nothing to do with the temperature began to spread through me. One corner at a time, I unfolded the cloth. It was a semi-automatic; I knew enough to know that but not much else. A little battered yet deadly all the same. I stared at its black lines while the large grip invited me to curl a hand and try it for size. I didn't, for it was in my mind that my first touch would complete the contract between myself and the pistol. Then I would have no option but to fulfil my part of the bargain. That I would have to go through with the plan. Up to that moment, that's all it was, a plan, a flight of imagination that could be discarded on the slightest whim. Now it was real, the pieces in place. All I had to do was keep my nerve. I exhaled. Hadn't realised I'd been holding my breath. Linnet laughed.

"You can touch it."

I nodded, curled my fingers around the butt and, still with it beneath the table, tested its weight. Heavier than I thought. But there was something very satisfying in holding it. Like I was born to it. Felt the smile on my face.

"You like?"

"Where did you get it?"

"Grandfather. He killed Germans in the war. Hated them."

She came a little closer. "Cut their ears off and strung them from a rafter in his barn."

I screwed up my face, stared at Linnet. Was she making fun? Don't know but she didn't blink. Maybe madness ran in the family. I touched the tip of my ear, making sure it was still there, but figured Linnet wanted more than souvenirs. I looked again at the gun, my gun. Mine as long as I wanted it. Could I use it? Could I point it at a man and pull the trigger? Truth was I didn't want to think about it. Guns had always been an alien concept. So "out there", I had never considered the use of one. All the things I'd done in the past, guns had never featured. The fact you could end a life with a single contraction of a finger muscle was too much to think about. Too much for a man who did his best to avoid confrontation.

Thoughts burned in my head. No. I began to wrap the piece back in its linen cover and tell

Linnet to take it back, that it wouldn't be needed, that I'd find a way of getting Felix's goods back without the use of a gun. But my words never made it out. From the corner of my eye I saw Linnick striding to our table.

A sick feeling bubbled in my guts. And then something more. Guess I'd just had enough.

As Ringo sat down opposite and rested his elbows on the table, I brought the gun from my lap, leaned forward so its bulk was hidden, and stuck the barrel in his chest. For the first time ever I saw something other than meanness register on his ugly face. A moment later, surprise over, it took on its usual deadpan aspect. Ringo didn't look at the gun but kept his eyes firmly on me. He pulled away, retreated from his confrontational stance. For my own part, I moved the gun back so that only the barrel was above the table. Ringo nodded.

"Good boy," he said. "You're learning." He almost sounded impressed. "One thing though," and again he came forward so our faces were only inches apart. "You should know who your friends are, and keep that for your enemies."

I spat out a laugh. "Friend?" I said.

"Friend," he repeated. "Thought you might like a little help." He pushed his jacket to one side. The butt of a pistol nestled in his waistband. Ringo's face showed nothing, was as soulless as a Hyena looking at fresh carrion. He jerked his chin at the gun, my gun. "But I see you're fixed up." I didn't reply. Seemed unnecessary.

He sat a while longer then moved his chair back. "We'll catch up later, Chance." He stood, and as if seeing her for the first time, tipped his head at Linnet. "Miss."

We watched him walk away, neither of us speaking until he disappeared to the street.

Jesus. I looked at the pistol in my hand, shook my head. Had I really held a gun on Ringo?

One thing though, and it was some satisfaction to realise, I'd been steady. I'd looked Ringo Linnick in the eye and not flinched. This gangster hard man thing – maybe I had a knack for it.

I moved the gun, pushed it into the back of my trousers, and caught Linnet staring. Her eyes sparkled. In fact her whole face glowed with a light I hadn't seen before. I wanted to fuck her. I mean, I really wanted to fuck her right there. She laid a hand on my wrist.

"You were amazing, Chance." Her whispered voice purred in my ear. "I knew you were the one."

Still fired with adrenaline, I said, "The one?"

She linked her arm around mine, pulled herself into my space. "The one to do things. You're not like the others, Chance. You think then act. The kind of man who calculates the odds and comes out ahead. I like that in a man." Oblivious to those around us, she licked my neck. "My kind of man."

I was ready to explode. Adrenaline, aggression, the fact I'd just stuck a gun in the face of a well-known hard man, I don't know, but endorphins were racing around my body like they'd hit the straight at Silverstone. Maybe I was that kind of man. I ran a hand along her thigh. She didn't resist.

"Maybe we should finish our drinks?" she said.

"And then?"

Linnet tipped her head to the exit. "I have an apartment on the waterfront."

I looked into her eyes, felt myself being pulled into her world, not caring if I ever got out.

Picking up my glass, I swallowed what remained, and put it on the table. "I'll call a cab."

*

"It's a Luger," I said. "A 9mm Parabellum." I sat at the table, holding the gun in both hands. Jimmy and Spence peered over my shoulder. They didn't speak. Didn't have to. They wanted to touch it, experience the thrill; feel the power of possession. Guess I felt sorry for them. It was mine. By deed and action I had made it my own. The incident with Ringo confirmed the gun had found its rightful owner. And if there were any doubts in my mind, Linnet had eased them. Boy had she eased them. In words and actions, Linnet knew exactly how to make a man feel like a man.

"They were issued to German troops during the war," I said, and held it aloft so they could see it better. Back at Linnet's apartment I'd read up on the gun. Wikipedia said it was classy and reliable, and I'd seen enough movies to recognise its distinctive shape. I weighed it in my hand, 2lbs of cold metal. Closing one eye, I squinted down the sight and swept the pistol across the room. I was Steve McQueen behind a blockhouse wall, taking aim on a convoy of trucks and motorcycles as they roared past. The image lasted until I remembered just who I was. In truth I was looking at a chipped and scratched antique, and a minimum of five years if caught in possession. Sometimes, reality can be a bitch. I glanced across at Linnet. She was perched on the couch, legs crossed at the ankle, a smile on her delicious face. I pulled myself together. Keep up the front. Reckoned I was doing a pretty good job.

"Bit old isn't it?"

I shrugged. "Still works."

"You've tried it then?"

I opened my mouth, quickly shut it. Jimmy was getting on my nerves. But he was right. I hadn't. Nor had I any intention of loosing off a few rounds. "Look," I said. "All we need do is wave it in Screwball's face. He'll shit a brick and give us the gear."

"But it is loaded? Just in case like."

I detached the clip. Showed him the bullets, then put it back, banging it home with the heel of my hand like I'd practised. Didn't want to look a fool. Making sure the safety was on, I placed it flat on the table.

"There won't be a 'just in case' scenario, Jimmy. That's to show," and I tipped my chin at the gun, "we mean business."

"And if they've got guns?"

49

The thought had occurred. The nightmare scenario where Screwball, George, and companions fronted me with an arsenal of weaponry, occurred every time I closed my eyes. And it was just me. Alone, unfettered by any kind of back-up, and waiting for an ending that would never make it into a story book. Maybe it was a metaphor for my life. Close, but no biscuit. I shook myself out of it, didn't want to think anymore.

"Look," I said. "We'll have the advantage. We go in, gun in hand, and won't give them a second to think. In and out in less than a minute." I spread my arms. "Job sorted."

Jimmy rubbed his chin. He flicked his head towards Linnet. "Where the fuck did she get it anyway?" He reached over my shoulder, fingers snaking towards the piece. I pushed it further away.

"Her granddad. Fought the Krauts in the war. Took it off a dead one." That's all I said. The mental image of Linnet's grandfather, bending over a corpse, sawing through the gristle of a dead soldier's ear, was too much.

Jimmy licked his lips. "When and where. How you gonna do it?"

"We, Jimmy. We." I twisted in my chair to look at him then turned my head to look at Spence. He hadn't said a word. From the moment I had entered the flat with Linnet and taken the gun from my pocket, he had remained silent. Occasionally he would lift his head, look at Linnet, then me, and then the gun. I shifted in my seat. I had showered, scrubbed myself clean back at Linnet's apartment, yet still felt uneasy. Somehow her scent lingered. She'd gotten inside me. I could smell her in my sweat, taste her in my mouth – and I wondered if Spence could tell, wondered if he knew. Waited for him to say something. But when I looked, he was back staring at the gun.

I swallowed, relieved he was oblivious to our betrayal. Of all the friends that had come and gone, Spence had remained constant. I shifted my eyes to Linnet. We really shouldn't have. I really shouldn't have. On the other hand, if he never found out... Couldn't help a smile creep on my face.

"I don't want it here."

I frowned. "What?"

"That thing." Spence poked the gun with a finger then pulled back as if he'd been stung.

"Take it away. I don't want anything to do with it." He moved from the table, took his coat from the back of the chair. "I'm going out," he said. "When I get back, I want it gone." He paused, and when he turned, sadness had spread over his face. "You too, Chance." He thought hard then nodded to himself. "I get back, want you and your stuff gone." He turned sharply, his voice a mumble as he disappeared down the hall. "Play your games somewhere else, Chance. Leave me out of it."

The door slammed. I sat in silence, stunned. Spence had never before let me down. My mistakes and misdemeanours never fazing, his loyalty unquestioning. Didn't deserve his friendship. Never had.

That was the low point, the point where I hit rock bottom. I saw the future. It was a hard, empty future of prison cells and death. Could have given up, nearly did. But a soft, cold hand on my neck eased my doubts. A spike of desire swept through me. Linnet. Sad to say, Spence was quickly forgotten, and I braced myself for what was to come. Linnet had that kind of effect. I patted her hand. Melancholy over.

"Well?" said Jimmy. Spence's defection passed without comment.

I took a breath. "They're going to have to do something with the gear," I said. "It's pure, undiluted. They'll have a place where they feel safe enough to cut it."

"And?"

"That's when they'll be at their most vulnerable." I paused, could hardly believe this was me, talking like I knew what I was doing. "We go in, take back what's ours."

"Just like that?"

"We have an advantage."

"We?"

I stared him straight in the eye. "Can't do this by myself, Jimmy."

He nodded. Reluctantly maybe, but at least he was in.

"So all we need to do is find out where their cutting room is?"

I picked up the Luger. Felt like I'd handled guns all my life. I could do this. All it required was confidence, balls, and a weapon that would make holes in anyone who stood in our way. I glanced at Linnet. There was a cold half-smile playing on her lips, and her nipples were hardening by the second. I swear this talk of gunplay was turning her on. She lifted her head, used a hand to sweep hair from her eyes. We held each other's gaze, our intimacy obvious for anyone willing to see. We had no secrets, she had told me everything. I looked back at the pistol.

"I know where it is," I said.

"What?"

Turning my eyes on Jimmy, I swept the gun round so it pointed at his chest. "Said I already know where it is."

7

Screwball's cutting room was in a quiet, suburban part of town. Leafy, residential; a place where nothing much ever happened. The house – three storeys and divided into flatlets – was sublet to students whose transitional nature made it an ideal base for the comings and goings of criminal enterprise. Nobody here saw anything. And if they did, they kept it to themselves.

Parked on the opposite side of the road, I gazed through the windscreen, jutted my chin at the building. "Which one?"

Sitting in the back, Linnet pushed her head between me and Jimmy, nodded at the house. I caught a tang of perfume. It flowed in a subtle blend of aromas that danced on my senses. Could almost taste her. Wanted to. Again.

"Basement flat."

She had insisted on coming, said without her we wouldn't know which apartment it was. I'd made a token protest, something about girls, guns, and the like. But it was weak, half-hearted. In truth, I liked having her around. Linnet gave me a reason to believe in what I was doing.

"Way in?"

She pointed. "Side door. Stairs on the right."

My chest heaved. More of her scent filtered through my nose. Felt myself drift. Not yet. Job first then Linnet. I glanced at her, the prize at the end of the line. Jimmy had offered me some speed. Just to keep going, he said. But with a gun in my pocket, I didn't want anything clouding my judgement. But once this was over I was going to bed for a week. Preferably with Linnet. Just had to keep it together a little longer. Because now was the time to act.

Ten minutes earlier, we had watched a grey Merc pull up outside the house. Screwball drove. Beside him, riding shotgun, was Pesca. He took a black sports holdall from the back seat, and followed Screwball into the house. When I saw the bag my pulse rate quickened. It was my bag. The one I'd travelled from Antigua with. The dogs hadn't even transferred the coke to another.

I checked my watch. Ten minutes was enough. Stroking the butt of the Luger, I glanced at

Jimmy. Scared shitless, he hadn't said anything since leaving Spence's flat.

"You ready for this?"

"Yeah." His voice betrayed him.

"Let's do it then."

I opened the car door, waited for Jimmy. Linnet was out before him. "Where're you going?"

"There." She pointed at the house.

"No way." I shook my head.

She arched an eyebrow and my vain attempt at chivalry died an unheroic death. She was the steadiest of us all. Calm, determined, I watched her walk towards the drive. Side-glanced Jimmy. Like me, his eyes were drawn to her ass and the way she moved. Didn't blame him, not at all, but a pang of possessiveness gripped me. I tapped him on the shoulder. "C'mon," I said. "Let's get it done."

We followed Linnet through an unkempt garden and past a wheel-less Ford Granada propped up on bricks. I looked up, checked the windows. No face looked down. No one in the street either. I took it as a sign of good fortune, and hurried forward, catching Linnet's hand as she was poised to ring the basement flat's bell. "There's a better way," I said and gently moved her aside. Starting with the buzzers for the top floor, I began to press them one at a time. On the fifth attempt, a tired voice answered.

"Yeah?"

I pressed the intercom. "Delivery."

The lock clicked and I pushed the door. So much for security, but hell, that's students. The hall was dark, shabby, ill-cared for. I took the lead, led them to the stairs, and descended the short flight to the basement. The door, second to the left as Linnet had said, was plain and unadorned except for a plastic number 2 on the top panel. Taking the gun from my waistband, and holding it at the port as if facing a duel, I stood to the side. Nodded to Linnet. We'd gone over this a dozen times, twice more in the car. Didn't matter, palms were sweaty, breathing shallow. Linnet made a fist and banged.

Now there was no going back. I tightened my grip on the pistol.

"Alex." Twice more she rapped on the door. "Alex," she said. Louder this time. Inside the room, something stirred. Whispered voices. Someone moved to the door.

"Who's there?" Heavy accent.

And then words. Words I couldn't understand, harsh syllables and vowels, flowed from

Linnet's mouth.

Behind the closed door a man answered in the same cut-throat way. A chain moved, a bolt slid back. Didn't dare breath. The door opened a crack. Heart pounded. Now. Should I do it now?

Screwball's puzzled voice came through the opening. "Linneska?"

I made it happen.

Like a marionette dancing to the puppeteer's tune, I stepped across, kicked back the door, and watched Screwball spin away. There was just time to see his startled face before I back-handed him with the pistol. Hands shot to his face as he went down. I moved in, swept the room with the gun, left to right and back again like I'd seen in those American cop shows. Jimmy and Linnet followed. The room was bare except for two long, decorator's tables and some folded chairs against the wall. Heavy drapes covered the only window. On one table: scales, a dozen packs of bicarb, jars of white powder that looked like talc. On the other, a shopkeeper's display of plastic baggies, tie-ups, and one brick-sized pack of pure, unadulterated cocaine. The black holdall lay open by the old cast fireplace. Rest of the drugs were still inside.

Screwball was on the floor, wiping blood from his nose. Behind the table, hands motionless, Pesca looked on. I moved the gun between them. To show I was serious, I pulled back the toggle lock and chambered a round. Screwball didn't move. I stared him down, didn't blink. A warning I wasn't playing games.

Even so a bead of sweat trickled down my face. And now the initial excitement was over, I realised how heavy the gun was. It began to waver in my hand. Thought I'd bull it out, show them who the boss was and thrust it forward. Somehow it just came out of my mouth. "Nobody move." Regretted it soon as it left my mouth. Sounded like a gangster in a 50s movie. A bad 50s movie.

Shit.

I glanced at Screwball. He was squinting, scrutinising my features, trying to read me. Could he? Could he guess my actions before I knew them myself? Had the impression that's what he was doing; wondering if I was capable of pulling the trigger and putting a bullet through his head. Or was he like me? Maybe he liked to work the odds. A second or two passed before he uncoiled himself from the floor. Screwball climbed to his feet, a stupid grin on his face. Guess he'd made up his mind.

He swept his arm around the room. "This what you want?"

Like a bad smell, the question hung in the air. Before I could come back at him with some tough guy shit, Screwball cut me dead. His voice was soft, almost sincere, but chilled me to the bone. "Then you have to take it. You put a gun on me, you have to use it. Can you? Can you shoot me?"

Bullseye. Could I pull the trigger? Could I shoot someone? Him? Sweat flowed freely down my back. The gun weaved in my hand. And Screwball knew. Knew what was in my mind, knew what I was thinking. Swear he did. His head jerked back, asked the question, how far was I prepared to go?

His grin widened for he was cock-sure of himself. "You want it," he pointed at his chest.

"You kill me." In an instant he was walking across the cutting room floor. One, two, three steps and he was almost upon me.

My finger tightened.

Jimmy was behind me. "Do it, Chance. For Christ's sake, drop him." His panic-flecked voice urged me to pull the trigger. His words echoed in my skull. Death was in my hand. All I had to do was...

But another voice countered. The one I had listened to all my life. Run, it said. Drop the gun and run till you're free of the nightmare. And then it was too late. Screwball was in my face, his big hand closing around the Luger, wrenching it from my grip. My world filled with him: his hateful eyes and spittle-flecked mouth; his crooked nose and garlic breath. He stared at me like a wild animal. Everything stopped as he held the gun aloft. Almost in slow motion, he began a forehand sweep with it at my head. I turned away, closed my eyes ready to feel the crack of bone. But a gunshot exploded behind me, and made everything that had gone before irrelevant.

The eruption of sound dulled my senses, felt like I was drowning. Was I hit? I looked down.

No flowers of red blossomed on my shirt. No holes anywhere that I could tell. And then I looked at Screwball. He had stopped dead, the pistol still raised like he was playing a childish game of statues. His expression hadn't changed but his eyes were glassy, distant, as if he saw something far away and was trying to focus. It was a place only he could see.

Another shot. Screwball twisted as the bullet butchered his insides. He fell like a discarded rag doll, dead before he hit the ground. That was the moment Pesca made a decision. The wrong one. He reached for the gun inside his jacket but before he could get a hand inside, a third shot obliterated his face. Pesca made a soft grunt, almost of resignation, folded in the middle and collapsed beneath the table. It was over in seconds.

I looked at Jimmy, then at Linnet. She held a gun; a Walther P .38. Another relic from the war. How many did she have? I had this mental image of her grandfather in the old country with a trunk full of weapons, and a ream of shrivelled ears dangling from the ceiling. I shook myself back to the present, looked at Screwball's lifeless body. Lifted my gaze to Linnet. "Thought he was your cousin?"

She dropped a shoulder, shrugged. "On my mother's side. Distant."

"You killed him."

"Yes."

I opened my mouth then quickly closed it. There really wasn't anything more to say. I took a big breath, stepped towards my bag.

"Da!"

I froze, looked back at Linnet, saw the gun pointed at my head. Fuck.

"Chimmy."

Jimmy met my gaze. Raised an eyebrow in an "all's fair in love and war" way, and casually shrugged. Double fuck.

"Get the bag, Chimmy."

He did as he was told, stepped over the lifeless Pesca, collected the pack of cocaine from the table, and picked up the holdall. As an afterthought, he took the Luger from the floor and put that in the bag too. I looked at Linnet. She held all the aces. Me? I had the joker and an empty feeling in my guts. I had played my last hand, been well and truly trumped, and was waiting to cash in my chips. Linnet's cold smile and hard heart burnt deep. I was a fool. But even as the thought came to me I realised, not as big a fool as Jimmy.

As he moved past, I reached out, tried to touch him before the barrel of Linnet's gun came between us. I raised my hands, no threat. Tried again. "Jimmy," I said. "Do this and Felix will never let you go."

He paused by the door. Just for a moment I thought he might grin, tell me it was all a joke.

But his instinct for humour had gone. He paused, thought to say something then changed his mind. What could he say? That he was sorry? That he was a lying bastard and deserved whatever Felix would bestow on him? No. There was nothing to say. He shuffled through the door with the holdall. Hoped I might never see him again. That may have been too much of a wish. Linnet still had the gun pointed at my heart. She had killed twice. Two that I knew of anyway. But the cold-blooded dispatch of her cousin and Pesca made me think there may have been more. Many more. I licked my lips; dry as ash. What next? Linnet didn't keep me waiting long. She held out her free hand.

"Keys."

Of course, car keys, my car. Why not use that too? I handed them over, carefully, and looked at her. Looked to see if anything was there; a hint of affection perhaps or an excuse that would help me understand. Like an "I'm sorry but I have to do this" or a "my life depends on it". There was nothing. Linnet pouted, dangled the keys in my face; even blew me a kiss. Think she was enjoying it. She backed out to the passageway, closed the door behind her.

I shut my eyes, let out a long, slow breath. Linnet had played me. From the first moment she had stalked, ambushed, and pounced. And I had put up as much fight as a tethered lamb. My gullibility astounded me. But the moment of crushing defeat passed quickly. Was in a better position than Screwball; I was still in the game, still standing. I opened my eyes, said a silent prayer of thanks to whatever god looks after the losers of the world, and scanned the room. Reality bit. A washed out drug factory and two corpses. And if I didn't recover the drugs by tomorrow, Felix McKenzie would see that I joined them.

Time to move.

Ears still ringing from the gunshots, I opened the door, peered out. Dark but empty. I hurried, made my way to the stairs, took them two at a time. Saw figures huddled around the stairwell at the top. Curious, unsure what the noise from the basement could be, and wondering what the fuck to do. I didn't waste time. Just lowered my head, and barged past. It would take a few minutes to discuss what they saw, what they heard. A few minutes to decide what to do. Investigate? Slink back to their rooms, pretend they never heard a thing? Then a few minutes more before the police were called. Useful minutes where I could make myself scarce.

Outside the sun was shining, birds singing. Sunlight slanted through the row of plane trees where my car had stood. I wracked my brain. Where would they go? Linnet's apartment was too obvious. They would have a plan, the need to get out of the city paramount. Too many people with big eyes and mouths. I was alive which meant if inclined, I could contact McKenzie and organise a manhunt. I wasn't inclined. Valued my life too much to tell Felix McKenzie what a fucking mess this was. London? The Big Smoke? Somewhere in my memory, pillow talk perhaps, I remembered Linnet talking about London. She had family there. I rubbed my chin. If they were going to London would they drive? Not in my car. Too many differentials: bailiffs, the police, or worse still, McKenzie's crew. Linnet's or Jimmy's? Jimmy's was known to Felix, and I wasn't sure whether Linnet even had a car? Hadn't seen one. Not even outside her apartment. Maybe a train? Lime Street station was little more than a fifteen minute ride away. Trains to London every hour. Checked my watch. In less than three hours they could be in London and lost for good.

The odds were stacking against me. It was a long shot, but every other permutation was worse. London then. I was putting everything on one card.

I started walking, hailed a cab and climbed in the back. The app on my phone showed me there was a London train departing in twenty-five minutes. "Lime Street," I said to the driver. "And quick. I've a train to catch."

8

I paid the cab fare, hurried inside the station. Beneath the roof's glass dome it was bright and sterile, the concourse thronged with commuters. I paused to look at the list of departures. London Euston was fourth from top – 14:47. Platform 7. Glanced at my watch, then across at the bay end terminus where a sleek Virgin Pendolino was already waiting.

Ten minutes.

Hope, the only thing I had, washed through me. Were they here? Or was this another hopeless gamble, a bet on the last race. Shit or bust. And how many times had that come off? Gnawed my lip. From the speaker above me, a robotic voice called out the latest departures. The waiting passengers moved to the gate like salmon on a spring tide.

I strained my neck, tried to see over heads. What if I was wrong? What if they were using a car, or had already gone? The last few days weighed heavy on me. Not only these last days but it seemed all the events of my life were pushing me towards this final act. Perhaps I should get on the train myself, leave it all behind. Fuck me. Leave what behind? All I had were bad debts and a broken relationship. Even Spence had turned his back on me.

I moved my head, looked through the glass doors. Sun was shining on the streets of

Liverpool. For all I had done, this city was my city. And unlike Spence, it would never turn its back on me. A wave of nostalgia flowed through me: the face in the bar, the laugh in the bookie's, the shout on the terraces, and the tears at the Shankly Gates. It was ingrained in blood and bone. I could leave Liverpool but Liverpool would never leave me.

I turned back, saw the Virgin Pendolino that could whisk me to a new life. It wasn't an option. I'd do what had to be done. And if not? Then the fish in the Mersey would feed well tomorrow.

Imbued with new determination, I looked again at the passengers. My breath caught. Passing the third car, her blonde bob telegraphing her presence like a beacon, was Linnet. She was prodding Jimmy in the back, pushing him up the step into a coach D.

Everything else was forgotten. I ran forward, pushed my way to the front of the queue.

"Ticket, sir."

"Sorry?"

"Ticket. Can't board without a ticket, sir."

I looked at the girl. Red coat, blue hat. Her name was Rebecca. The tag had a flourish and the word Virgin beneath. I searched her eyes, opened my mouth ready to charm her with some old flannel but saw the steely resolve within. Instead I stammered, pointed at the train a few metres away. "Just seeing someone off."

A saccharine smile stretched her lips and she scrunched her face in what someone at development probably called cute but forceful. "Sorry, sir. Can't enter the platform without a valid ticket."

Should I try the ogre instead? But Rebecca was made of strong stuff. I could tell, and her colleague was casting me looks that would curdle milk.

"Could you move back please, sir. You're blocking the gate."

I held up my hands, allowed myself to drift back on an eddy of humanity. Had to think. If I didn't move fast, I'd be waving goodbye to eight kilos of the white stuff, and probably my bollocks as well. Back of the queue, I weighed my options. A glass barrier ran the length of the platform separating the eleven coaches of the train from the concourse. On my side, cash machines and the Virgin ticket office. No cash and no time for a ticket. But the barrier was only waist high. Wouldn't take much to climb over. Decision made, I hurried to the ticket office but instead of going in, swerved from the door and continued along the concourse until opposite the driver's cab of the train. No one here except a couple of spotters taking numbers. I jumped the barrier, walked quickly along the platform, and boarded the train into first class.

Just in time, the doors closed. The take-up was smooth,

hardly seemed we were moving. And while the outside world darkened as we entered the cut towards Edge Hill, I took a breath, thought about what I was doing. This was it. We were on our way to London. Just prayed I might think of something before we arrived.

Starting to walk, I counted off the carriages. Two first class then through the buffet. Three, four. At five I slowed, peered through the sliding doors. Did the same at six. At seven I was even more cautious. It was coach D.

I glanced along its length. They were just inside, had a table seat to themselves. Jimmy facing, Linnet her back to me. I ducked back into the vestibule lest Jimmy see. But I had little to fear. He was completely absorbed in Linnet.

What now? I had no plan, no thought on how to separate Jimmy from Linnet, and Linnet from the drugs. Once I would have sat and waited; waited for something to happen, something to turn up. But that was then. If I was to achieve anything, I had to make it happen. But without a plan that was little comfort. From the speaker above my head, a flat voice announced: "This train is for London, calling at..." Four stops. I looked at my watch. If I didn't think of something, in a little over two hours, they'd be gone forever. Ran a hand through my hair. Came back slicked with sweat. Behind was the toilet. Freshen up and think. Time I had, a couple of hours before we reached the Big Smoke anyway.

The door closed and I waited for the electronic lock to engage before looking in the mirror.

Christ, I looked like a tramp. Tried the tap. Water trickled out, tepid and greasy, but I filled the sink, and splashed my face. How the fuck was I to get my hands on the gear?

Before any thoughts formed, the door hissed open. Turned my head. The train manager, a fat man with a double chin and paunch that looked like he had swallowed a football, stood in the opening. His mouth dropped. His chins wobbled. For a moment he couldn't speak then a ream of apologies gushed. "I am sorry, sir," He stammered. "I... I had no idea anyone was here."

I showed him my wet hands. "Just washing," I said. "No harm done." I gave him my "everything is fine and dandy" smile and prayed he didn't ask to see my ticket.

"Even so," he said, shaking his head. "Should have knocked,

called out. Lock's broken see, sir." In way of explanation, he held out an Out of Use notice for me to see. "Though you can't tell from inside. You could," and he ran a finger around the inside of his collar, "be doing something, see, and whoosh!" His hands sprang apart. "Door just opens. Had problems on the way up see. These electric things." He made a "what can you do about it" face, and shook his head. "Better with a simple bolt, like they used to have. Don't know why they keep having to change things, really don't. Anyway," he said, flourishing the notice again. "Someone should have put this in place before we set out. But one thing and another. A lot of things need sorting before the train departs, sir."

What he meant was he should have put the notice up. Guy was in the shit, thinking I might report him. Good. Advantage me. "It's not a problem," I said. "Really."

His face relaxed. "Very understanding, sir."

I took a couple of paper towels from the dispenser and dried my hands.

"They'll sort it once we get to London," he said. "In the meantime..."

"I'll use another," I said. "If I need to."

"Thank you, sir. Thank you."

I squeezed past; made to make for the seat I never had, and waited while he peeled off the paper backing, and stuck the notice to the outside of the door. After he disappeared, I went back, tried the open and close buttons just to be sure, then sat in the vestibule.

An idea was beginning to form.

*

We were halfway to Crewe when my opportunity arrived. From my position, I could see Linnet and Jimmy without them seeing me. Eventually it happened. Jimmy whispered to Linnet and got out of his seat. He needed to piss. I moved quickly, peeled off the Out of Use notice from the toilet door, and slipped to the other side. Pressed in the cavity beside the exit, I heard the door slide open, shut, and the lock engage. But unlike Jimmy, knew it didn't work. No second thoughts this time. Couldn't afford the slightest hesitation. Lifting the fire extinguisher from the bracket in the space beside me, I cradled it in the crook of my arm, and went to the toilet door. It was small, but heavy enough to do the job. I counted to five, and pressed open.

Dick in hand, Jimmy looked up from the toilet bowl. His surprise was beginning to turn from indignation to comprehension that my appearance was not a good thing, and perhaps he should do something about it, when I rammed the flat-bottomed end of the extinguisher in his face. There was a crack as steel met bone. I dropped the extinguisher as the shock wave powered up my arm, and watched Jimmy stagger back. He crashed into the wall and slid down, head resting on the toilet seat. I closed the door, looked him over.

There was a large red ring stretching from forehead to chin, taking in a nose that was now a different shape than before. He didn't move. Checked his pockets. No gun or ticket. Guessed Linnet was keeping those to herself. So far no one had tried the door. Perhaps my luck had changed. But I wasn't counting on it, and knew I had to be quick. Pushing my ear to the door I heard nothing but the train's gentle rattle. Stepping out smartly, I closed the door, and stuck the Out of Use sign back on the panel.

I was feeling better than I had in a long time, when I slid into the seat opposite Linnet.

Those big eyes opened a touch wider as she realised it was me and not some loser making a move on her. But she settled back, regained her composure quicker than I liked, and smiled that smile that had men falling at her feet. Wasn't sure whether I wanted to slap her or fuck her.

"Chimmy?" she asked.

"Engaged," I said.

She nodded as if this were no great surprise, and pushed a hand towards her bag on the seat.

I got to it first, moved it out of reach. It was the Louis Vuitton I had seen the day before. Inside was the Walther P .38. I went to take it, remembered it had killed two men, and left it where it was. Didn't want to touch it. I'd had my fill of guns. I snapped back the clasp and pushed it behind me.

"That mine?" I said and jerked my chin at the black sports holdall on the rack above her head.

"Yours?" She raised an eyebrow.

"For the purposes of this conversation," I said, "yes."

She leaned across the table, placed an elbow on the surface and rested her chin in her hand.

Her perfume wafted towards me. Beneath the table, her leg brushed mine.

"The bag," she said, "may be yours. But the contents," she shrugged, "belong to someone else."

Linnet waited, willing me to concede I was a nobody, a pawn in a game played by others.

But I had no intention of amusing her. "That's no concern of yours. Let's say, the gentleman concerned would not be happy if it were to go missing – again."

Linnet smirked and sat back. She stared at me, toyed with a gold bracelet on her wrist. "How did you know?"

"Know?"

"This." She raised a hand and circled the air. "The train. This train."

"You've said it before. I play the percentages, look for the best return." I shrugged. "Lucky guess."

She shook her head. "No. I think you are a very clever man, Mr Chance." Beneath the table she scissored my legs, tightened her grip, levered herself forward so her face was inches from mine. "Should have known it would be you, not Chimmy. Should have known to trust you."

Linnet reached out a hand, her fingers playing with a button on my shirt. I caught her wrist.

Not this time. She wasn't going to play me again. "So Jimmy was just a means to get what you wanted?"

She shrugged. "A girl has to do…"

"And when you have what you want, you discard what you don't need? When were you planning to dump Jimmy?" I almost felt sorry for the two-faced bastard.

Linnet frowned. Could almost see the cogs moving inside her head. Her usual methods of seduction weren't working. She tried something else. "Look," she said. "We'll be in London in two hours. I know people, I have family…"

"Like Screwball?"

She straightened her back, indignant. "Not like him. Different." She bobbed her head at the rack and my bag. "That's a passport to whatever we want. But I can't do it by myself, Chance. You know its value." And she lowered her voice. "But it's pure, unadulterated. If we were to cut and market it ourselves..." She raised her eyebrows expectantly. "Would you know the street value then?"

Yeah. I knew only too well. I opened my mouth, closed it, and she saw temptation stretched on my face as a million tiny £ signs fluttered in front of my eyes.

"Half a million, Chance. Each. You don't have to like me." Again that "but how could you not like me" smile. "But we can work it out. I know we can. We could go anywhere, do anything."

She was staring, pushing herself forward, hoping to twist me to her way of thinking. I broke the connection, looked out the window. Green fields, hedges; we crossed a bridge over a lazy river. Postcard pretty and as different from the dark conurbations of home as it could possibly be.

She saw me, maybe saw something else too. Something I wasn't even aware of. "With your share you could buy your own place, Chance. Maybe in the country? I mean, what have you got in Liverpool?"

I met her steely gaze with one of my own. "One thing I don't have is a price on my head.

But if I were to venture into an independent franchise with you, a certain gentleman would leave no stone unturned in his quest to rip off my balls and stuff them down my throat. Besides I'm a city boy." I tapped the glass with a nail. "Too much fresh air can make you ill."

"Please," She reached out, stroked my hand. "Please, Chance. I know you." She smiled. "I know what you like. We could go somewhere, now. Get off at the next stop and talk." She paused and again that smile. "Well, talk after, I mean."

Her touch was poison. I thought of Screwball and Jimmy, nameless others she'd used, and the way she had shafted me. Looked her straight in the eye. "I don't believe you, Linnet. You're like Ebola. Anything comes in contact with your bodily fluids is fucked. So no. Thanks very much but I'll pass."

The change was instant. There was ice in her eyes, and murder in her heart. If she could have dropped me dead with one look, she would have done so. Linnet tensed as I stood and took the holdall from the rack above her head. Outside, the suburbs of Crewe were slipping past the window. The train slowed, and I shuffled around the table, bag in hand.

"Have a nice life," I said, and the devil in me couldn't help but add, "with Chimmy." For the first time in days, felt like I was winning. My aches and pains, the trauma of the recent past, dissolved into the ether as if I'd taken some magic pill.

Crewe. The train stopped and I jumped down to the platform. Looked at the bag in my hand.

The shackles that tied me to it, if not broken, had loosened considerably. I had it. It was mine. And it wasn't leaving my side until I handed it to Felix. I needed to get home. But I waited, didn't move until I scanned the entire length of the train. I was taking no chances. If Linnet put so much as a foot outside the door, I would kick her back on. Fuck the consequences. But there was no sign of her. As it pulled out, I stepped back, watched it all the way until the red tail lamp was a pinprick winking in the distance. Next stop was Stafford. If she wanted to come back at me then, it would be too late. I'd be halfway to Liverpool.

I allowed myself a smile, gripped the handle of the holdall, felt the weight lift from my shoulders. Next train to Liverpool was ten minutes.

Crossing the bridge, I settled myself on a bench away from other passengers. Didn't want to talk, didn't want to get stuck in a loop of meaningless conversation with people who meant nothing to me. I looked along the flat curve of platform and stonewashed buildings. Needn't have worried. People were lost in their own worlds, texting faceless colleagues, or talking into mobile phones. Maybe it was an excuse not to mingle with their fellow travellers. Maybe alone was the human condition. Maybe...

Shut up, Chance. Stop thinking. I smiled, and grateful for the advice, closed my eyes. Jesus.

How had I got in such a mess? But I was nearly there now, light at the end of the tunnel. Felt I could sleep for a week.

I was glancing at the destination board for the hundredth time, when I saw her.

Shit.

Linnet was walking the access between platforms, flanked by two Transport Police. I jumped like the bench was on fire. How the fuck...? No time. She had seen, was pointing, and a cop walking over. The world tilted. Thrown into confusion, I looked for escape. Police one way, tracks the other. Heart hammered. A

66

rat-trap. I gripped the bag tighter. Eight kilos of the white stuff and a year for every kilo if they searched it. Or did Linnet have a plan? Take back her holdall and do me for nothing more than nicking her bag? Maybe she wouldn't press charges, claim she didn't want the hassle. Who cared. I wasn't giving it up. Not now. I started backing away. The cop raised a hand.

"You."

It was enough. I broke forward, teetered on the platform edge, saw the Liverpool train rounding the curve, and jumped just as the cop's authoritative voice broke into a shriek. His strangulated cry was lost in a squeal of brakes. "Stand clear, stand clear." Warm locomotive breath seared my neck, rancid fumes filled my nostrils, while the throb of the huge diesel engine reverberated through my skull like the last clarion call. I stumbled, nearly lost my foot beneath the metal monster, but had nothing to lose. This was endgame. I rolled, barely escaped the wheels, and sprinted across the lines. Slow, fast; up line, down line, the Feds wouldn't take me without a fight. Sights and sounds, too many to process, crowded my brain. But I was blinkered, saw only what I wanted – escape, and didn't stop until I got there.

On the other side of the tracks, I hurled the holdall over the lip of the platform, and hauled myself after it. For a minute I was safe. Crouched by the stairs of the over-bridge, had time to stop and look. No pursuit. Not yet anyway, and for a moment was hidden from view by the train I'd ran in front. A precious few seconds were mine. But it wouldn't last. Then the dogs would run me to ground.

My lungs ached, sweat ran down my face, but the fear had gone. Now it was purely a race – hare and hounds, escape or capture. Behind I could hear the grind of wheels as the train began to move. Had to keep going. It was my only hand. Ahead were the station offices. Between one set and another, I could see steps leading to an area of wasteland. I went for it, scrambled down. Beneath fern and briar were old rusted tracks. Greenery sprouted between the sleepers. I ran, fell, got up and kept running. Still no sign of the bizzies and a minute later, was on the other side, clambering up into the old parcel depot. It led to a shale track and a series of refurbished buildings. In front was a sign: "Traction Training Depot. Private".

It was quiet. A scatter of rail vans and cars sat by the workshops. Birds sang. No time to take in the scenery, just move. I wiped my face on a sleeve, started walking. Long strides propelled me past the buildings; was going well but an open door made me pause. Going over, I cocked my head, listened, eased the door back. Bags, coats on pegs, boots on floor. A few incoherent voices mumbled through the wall. I took a sleeveless high-visibility jacket with Network Rail logos, and a white safety helmet from a peg. Outside I put them on, sauntered up the hill, bag slung over my shoulder, and headed to the road. Cutting right, I made my way to the station's main entrance.

Before going in, I dialled 999 on my mobile phone, told the police operator there was a woman: blonde hair, slim figure, and carrying a white Louis Vuitton bag, on the station concourse. She had a gun and was prepared to use it. Then I broke the connection.

I gave it a few minutes, then walked down the steps to the bay platform and Chester train on platform 9. I passed the barrier with no more than a smile, just an off-duty railman on his way home. Going via Chester was a bit of a detour, but I figured if the police were still looking, they wouldn't think I'd take the longer route. Besides, they were busy with another matter. Linnet was face down on the floor, surrounded by a posse of armed police. I gave them a wide berth, sat on the train, and didn't move until the doors shut, and we rattled away. Finally I dared look. Still on the floor, Linnet was being frisked by a cop who seemed to be enjoying his task more than he should. As the train passed, its engines belched a fume of exhaust. When it cleared, Linnet had latched onto my face like a magnet does metal. She didn't move but her eyes followed, and I pressed my nose against the glass, watching all the way until we rounded a curve and she was lost from sight. Did I feel anything? Nothing. Zilch. Absolute zero. My passion had expired on a web of deceit and lies. I sat back, counted the miles between us. Hoped she'd share a nice cold cell with a lesbian weight lifter.

It was twenty minutes to Chester, another forty to Liverpool. No one asked to see my ticket.

The Network Rail jacket was an all areas pass, and I waltzed through the barriers at Central like a roadie at Glastonbury.

Circling the surrounding streets, I eventually found my car, threw the parking ticket in the gutter, and set off back to the apartment. I'd hit the home straight. Shit, shower, shave; then make the delivery to Felix. What could possibly go wrong now?

9

Should have known something was wrong when I saw the door. It was open. Not much, but enough to notice. Pushed it with my foot, "Spence," I said, and stuck my head in. No reply. The silence was tangible, felt like the apartment was holding its breath waiting for me to enter. Instinct told me to turn and head in the opposite direction, fast. Cut and run, my usual method of operation. But what about Spence? Couldn't let him down again. Guessed I owed him that much.

I moved forward quietly, found Spence lying on the living room floor. There was blood on his temple and he wasn't moving. Further back, sitting in an armchair, was George. And the gun in his hand was pointed at my head. George didn't speak. Didn't have to. The gun and his eyes said everything I needed to know.

The breath caught in my throat.

George waved the gun, called me to the centre of the room. Glanced at Spence. How bad did

I feel bringing this shit on him? Bad. But not as bad as the feeling I got when I looked at George. His face was set in a cold, no-nonsense way, and I knew better than to argue. Truth was, my mind was running, looking for an edge to somehow get out of this mess, and still be standing at the end of it. Seemed like George knew what I was thinking for he shook his head. And no matter how many permutations ran through my mind, I couldn't see a way out. If I'd been placing a bet in the bookie's, I would have walked away, kept my money.

But I wasn't placing a bet. I was gambling on my life. And the odds were stacked against me.

I stared at George, waited while he shifted in his seat, and settled back making himself more comfortable. "You got it then?" He jutted his chin to the holdall in my hand.

"It?" I was stalling, playing for time. George knew exactly what I was doing.

"Don't play games," he said. "I want the coke, that's all."

"And?"

He shrugged. "Then you can get on with your life."

Get on with my life. A life that would probably end with a bullet to the brain. And whether it was George or Felix McKenzie who pulled the trigger was, at that moment, not a great priority.

I dropped the holdall, cleared my throat. "Maybe we can come to some arrangement. There's enough for both of us." Touched the bag with my foot. "We can split it. Fifty-fifty." It was the same offer Linnet had made me. And I had about as much to bargain with.

George smirked. "And you're offering?"

I opened my mouth, shut it quickly.

George laughed. Laughed at me, laughed at my predicament. It was deep and came from some dark place where humour was a tool to be used like any other. "In case you hadn't noticed," he said, and wagged the gun in his hand. "I have this. And you have..."

Nothing. That's what I had. I was a lame horse on the gallops, waiting for a bullet to put me out of my misery.

"Use your foot and slide the bag over. And keep your hands where I can see them."

I looked at the holdall, realised I'd finally run out of luck. Putting my trainer on the holdall, I was about to side-foot it across the room when he stopped me.

"Wait." He pointed to the floor with his free hand. "Open it. Let me see."

I squatted, ran the zip along the centre. As the bag parted, my breath caught. On top of the drugs, just as Jimmy left it, was the Luger. George never took his eyes from my face, reasoning any attempt to escape would show there first. But I'd played poker with the best, knew how to keep a straight face. There was one chance to break the bank. Reaching in, I made it look like I was bringing out the packs of drugs. Instead I lifted out the pistol and pointed it at George. Couldn't remember whether it was loaded, whether I'd chambered a round or the safety was off. But at that moment it was the most beautiful of things.

George never moved. One minute he was holding the winning hand, ready to cash in. The next, we were in some kind of Mexican standoff, the conclusion of which was still in doubt.

"So," he said. "You do have something to bargain with." He

paused for effect. "You're right, there is plenty for two." He eased the hammer back on the pistol, moved it a fraction from where it pointed. "Maybe we can do a deal."

I looked at George, he looked at me, stared at me in fact, a sneer not far from his face. Too easy, and I knew it wouldn't end like this. Even if I got out of this alive he'd pursue me to the grave. Like a dog with a bone, George would never let go. He would take it personally, the insult burning into his psyche as a judgement on his manhood. Daryl Chancellor, the man who played the odds and beat him. And I'd live the rest of my days looking behind me, waiting for a tap on the shoulder and a bullet in the head. Chance of a successful outcome? 3/1 against at best. That's what I thought anyway. So I shot him. Twice. And as he lay on the floor twitching, and going into convulsions, I shot him again. Through the head.

He wouldn't be following anyone after that.

10

Spence looked at his beer. Had been looking for some time. He had a black eye and a lump on his head the size of an egg. "That's it," I said. "The whole story." I shrugged. "Nothing to add." I took a sip of beer, eyed Spence over the rim of the glass. Except there was. Lots.

We stood in a corner of Rigby's, leaning on the wooden counter, apart from the life going on around us. Maybe it was our aura, maybe it was our bruised and battered faces that caused the rest of the punters to give us a wide berth. But we were left alone, left to stew in our privacy. I bought the first beers, drank mine too quickly then waited for Spence to catch up and get the next round. I was sticking to Wychwood, good English ale. Anything exotic was right off the list. We had been quiet, circling each other; wary, embarrassed even, exchanging small talk, unable to look the other in the eye until the second beer lubricated my vocal chords and I told him everything. Most of it anyway. But there are some things best left unsaid. Like the part where me and Linnet... Well, you get the picture?

A moment or two passed while I waited for Spence to say something. Anything. He shuffled his feet, rubbed his chin.

"She was a tramp, Spence. You're better off without her."

He nodded, slow and precise, agreeing with my assessment but wishing it wasn't so. He lifted his glass, paused before it reached his mouth. "George," he said. "How did you...?"

I held up a hand. "Best you don't know."

"Even so."

"Yeah," I said. "Sorry about the mess and everything."

Spence frowned. "Did you," he hesitated, afraid to ask. "Kill him?"

"Christ, Spence. Who d'you think I am?" He opened his mouth, but I got in first. "When I saw the open door, I crept in and gave him a whack pretty much the way he did you. Didn't know what hit him." I gulped at my beer.

"And?"

"Dumped him in the alley next to the pool club. After that..." I shrugged. "Someone else's problem." What I didn't tell Spence was the trouble I had getting George's body down the stairs and in the car without being seen. Dumping him in the river was the easy part. And if he ever surfaced – well George had plenty of enemies. Spence would never know. Not from me anyway.

He went back to his beer. Sipped slowly. "What about McKenzie? You done the," he made a face, "thing?"

"Drop?" I was getting good with the terminology. "Did it this morning." In truth, I was glad to be rid of the frigging stuff.

"Did he pay you?"

I shifted uncomfortably, the memory still raw. Felix and two of his goons had been there. He didn't say a word. Just watched me put the packs of coke on his table; then watched me all the way out. Shook my head.

"You got nothing?" Spence's face creased like he felt it personally.

"Suppose I'm lucky to get away with me balls still attached. One of his boys said I'll be seen right. But I'm not holding my breath."

I took a swallow of beer, looked at the glass. Down to the final dregs. In my pocket were a few coins, not even enough for another round. I looked at Spence, then at my glass. Wondered if he'd get the hint. Subtlety was never my speciality, so I drained what was left and thumped the glass down on the counter. Glanced at Spence, had raised my eyes to his face expectantly when a shadow fell across the bar. Spence's face drained of colour. I turned my head.

Ringo Linnick stood behind me.

Spence pushed himself further into the corner. I stood my ground. Wasn't going to run, not anymore. Had done enough of that. Even so, I winced as Ringo's heavy hand landed on my shoulder. "Relax, Chance," he said. "Just here to talk."

His big fingers probed until he found the soft spot he was looking for. He squeezed, hard.

Pain shot through me like an electric bolt. Ringo patted me like a favourite hound, seemed to find it amusing.

Rubbed my shoulder. "Ringo," I said. "I'm good for the money. Really am this time."

Leaned close to his ear. "Deal's gone down, just waiting the payoff."

Ringo held up his hands. "It's okay, Chance." Ringo never smiled, not really. The best he got was a thin line that somehow made his face less forbidding. But smile he did. "I've been sent to tell you, your debt's written off."

I froze. Something was wrong with my hearing. "What?"

"I said your debt's clear. Paid in full."

I snorted a laugh, waited the punchline.

"It's true," said Ringo. Word of honour."

Still I waited.

"Look if you don't believe." Ringo reached into his jacket and I tensed at the thought of what he might be reaching for. But it was merely a book – his book. The book that bore the name of every debtor this side of the Mersey. He thumbed the pages until he found what he wanted. Ringo pushed it under my nose. "See."

I looked over his hand. It was true. There was my name and a pen strike through the entry.

Written in green biro and capital letters was the single word – Paid.

Ringo waited while the information filtered into my brain then snapped the book shut. Didn't want me seeing too much. It disappeared back in the folds of his coat. "Thought you'd like to know," he said.

He turned, had started to move away, when he stopped and slapped the counter with his hand. "Almost forgot," he said. Reaching into his trouser pocket, Ringo brought out his wallet. Prising it open, he took out a £10 note and laid it on the bar. "Mr

McKenzie, said I should give you this. Said a promise is a promise, and he wouldn't like you to go short." He saw my face. For a moment I thought he was going to laugh. Lines appeared beneath his eyes, and the corners of his mouth turned up. But that would have been too much, and a second later, his face returned to stony neutrality. Ringo turned his back, flicked a hand above his head. "See you around, Chance."

I watched him go, felt the nausea rising, and closed my eyes. What a dick I'd been. Working my arse off, keeping my head above water and my balls intact to pay back a debt to the bloke who lent me the money in the first place. I looked at the £10 note. The payoff. I lifted it from the counter, turned it in my hands as if it would burn. That was it, ten quid. All that shit and ten quid.

Spence finally let out a breathe. "Jeez, that was close." He paused then nodded at the money, his natural optimism quickly returning. "Well at least you can get the next round in."

I nodded. "Yeah, I could," I said slowly and rubbed my chin. "Can you get them, Spence?

Thing is, there's a dead cert running in the 3.10 at Wincanton. Can't lose." I held the £10 out for him to see. "This is all I've got," I said, and felt my heart begin to beat just that touch faster. Gave him my best smile. "Unless you can lend us fifty quid, that is."

Always and Forever

Jason Weever stared at the rain. Since leaving Kings Cross it hadn't stopped. Not once. It splattered against the window and ran towards the sill leaving dirty rivulets on the glass outside. Jason watched, and as he did, he pondered the force of nature that drove some to the left, and some to the right. It was the only thing that occupied his tired mind.

He left the express at Leeds, crossed the footbridge, and boarded the two-car diesel that would take him on the Settle–Carlisle line. Once more he gazed through the window. And with each passing town, each church spire and black-water canal, his lassitude grew. Only when the hills and moors of the Dales filled his vision did a spark of interest finally flicker. But still the rain fell.

Jason nearly missed his stop. The train slowed, the station board slipped by and in a fit of panic, he grabbed his bags, and darted through the door just before they closed. Behind him the train clattered away. He was the only one to alight. Jason put down his bags and looked at the land. It seemed to soar around him: brown scrub and dry-stone walls, tumbling becks and lonely farms. On the embankment above the station, sleepers had been up-ended and hammered into the slope to keep snow off the line. A cold wind blew off the moors. Jason shivered. Dent – the highest station in England. Late October; he could only imagine what it was like in the depths of winter. Jason nodded. He had chosen well.

Picking up his holdall, Jason turned and looked over his new home. Fully refurbished and described in the brochure as "Derby Gothic", the twin-gabled station house was privately owned and being leased as a holiday cottage. Just as they said, the key was beneath a pot on the step. Turning the lock, Jason pushed open the door. A feeling of time preserved in aspic flowed from within. Beneath the fresh paint and turpentine, he caught the aroma of age, of stone and earth, and long-kept secrets. Maybe even a trace of those gone before. For a moment he stood on the step lost in the past. Then he closed his eyes and breathed the heady mixture. It lasted seconds before reality asserted itself and he entered the hall. A flagstone floor led left to the lounge and right to the master bedroom. On the opposite wall, an oval mirror, and a door that led to the kitchen. Jason went through. It was clean and bright with pine cupboards and chequered tiles. Placing his bag on the table, Jason walked to the window and looked over the fells. Empty, bleak, lonely. A long sigh of satisfaction escaped Jason's lips. Yes, he had chosen well.

That first night Jason lit the Rayburn and revelled in the silence. Only the wind raking the moors broke his thoughts. In the early hours a freight train rumbled past. Rising from his bed, he brushed the curtain aside and peered out. It was a heavily laden coal train bound for the power station at Drax. Broken shadows flailed the darkness and Jason watched long after it was gone and its single red light dipped out of sight. He dropped the curtain and returned to bed. For the first time in a long while, he slept till dawn.

*

After three days with only the hourly train service and the odd hiker for company, the need for civilisation was uppermost in Jason's mind.

Though giving its name to the station, Dent was a little more than four miles distant. It was a pretty village of stone cottages, cobbled streets, a couple of pubs and not much else. Jason bought pasta, mince and eggs from the general store then began to walk back. Halfway along Main Street he stopped. The door of The George and Dragon was open, and he hesitated only briefly before going in. Inside it was cosy, traditional; dark wood panels and brown leather seating. In the lounge, a plasma TV tuned to Sky News, was fixed to one wall while the bar stood at the other. Sitting at the far end, was a bored-looking kid in his early twenties. He had squeezed his bulk onto a narrow-backed stool, and leaning forwards, the crack of his arse showed over his pants. He was half listening to the barmaid, and from the look on his face, she was telling him things he didn't want to hear. As Jason entered, he flicked greasy hair out of his eyes and looked him over. The girl smiled and walked across.

Jason looked at the beer pumps. "What's good?"

"Apart from me?" she said and raised a smile until a derisory grunt from the boy washed it from her face. She cut him a sidelong glance then turned back to Jason.

Her skin was pale, almost translucent, and Jason found himself drawn to her brown eyes that gazed at him in a manner he found a little disconcerting. She reminded him of the kids he saw in London, hanging around Euston or Kings Cross, begging for change. They lived on the margins of society, almost on a separate plane, as if their peripheral existence were out of kilter with a world they had no place in. Jason often felt the same way, kindred spirits, as it were. This girl had the same quality.

She lifted a hand to push a strand of hair out of her eyes. "Dark or light?"

"Dark."

"Aviator," she said and stretched for a glass on the shelf above. Her small breasts pushed at the thin material of her vest top. She began to pour. "Passing through?"

"I'm stopping a while." Jason said and pulled a stool to the bar. "I'm renting the old station house."

"Bit quiet up there isn't it?"

"Suits me," he said and handed over a note.

She made a face and went to the till. "Just you?"

He nodded. "Just me."

Her eyes settled on Jason's face as she handed him his change. "Must be lonely," she said, "by yourself, I mean?"

"Christ!" The boy at the end of the bar had heard enough. He scraped back his stool and stalked from the room. As he passed, he deliberately brushed Jason's elbow, jerking the glass in his hand. Beer slopped onto the bar. The girl's face clouded. She reached for a cloth and began to wipe the counter.

Jason put his glass down. "Boyfriend?"

"Thinks he is."

"But you're not sure?"

She stopped what she was doing and looked hard at Jason. "Oh I'm sure all right." Not wanting to get involved he raised his hands defensively. The girl went back to wiping down the counter, making big, circular motions with the cloth.

"Don't mind Wayne," she said, "he just gets..."

"Jealous?"

She looked skywards. "Protective."

Jason went back to his beer.

"So is it?"

"Is it what?"

"Lonely," she said, "by yourself?"

Jason stared across the bar. From the back room he could hear the clack of balls from the pool table. He lifted his glass. "Like I said before, it suits."

She was about to say more but on the other side of the bar, Wayne's face appeared at the hatch. He banged his empty glass on the bar. "'Nother pint, Lyza."

"Lyza," said Jason. "Like Minnelli?"

She scrunched up her face. "Sort of."

Jason nodded and slid off the stool. He finished his beer and picked up his bag.

"See you again?" she said.

"I guess."

Lyza waited.

Taking the hint, Jason paused by the door. "Jason," he said. "But most of my friends call me Jay."

Lyza smiled. "Okay, Jay."

Wayne's glass rapped the counter again. "Come on, Lyza. Dying of thirst here."

Her soft eyes widened. Then slowly, very slowly, she walked across and snatched the glass from his fat fingers.

Outside it was raining. In the short time Jason had been in the pub, black clouds had swept over the valley and darkened the sky. Jason started to walk. And with each step he cursed himself for a fool. Why had he done it? Why had he opened himself to scrutiny, and a familiarity he didn't want? He wouldn't let it happen – not this time. But as he walked the long road home, it was hard to get Lyza out of his mind.

*

Next day Jason woke early. Determined to make his lethargy a thing of the past, he found his backpack, made a flask of coffee and set off onto the moors.

From wet and miserable to crisp and golden, the weather had broken. Soft-edged clouds, like sheep in a field of opal blue, meandered slowly towards the horizon. The air was sharp, pure, and suffused with the earth's rich aromas. Jason followed the road to Cowgill, and then a narrow track to Arten Gill viaduct. Passing under the structure, he started to climb. As he gained height, the land changed. Long, coarse grass gave way to thinner, flat vegetation. Heather and tufted hummocks proved dry stepping-stones while the land between squelched beneath his boots. The wind was on his face, and the sweet smell of the earth filled his nostrils. It felt good. Halfway to the ridge he stopped to look back. The contours of the hills had a soft, undulating aspect that reminded him of a sleeping woman. And the thought came to him that if he trod softly, if he moved without noise, he could pass by without anyone ever knowing he had come that way. Jason sighed. It was something he had tried to achieve all his life. Turning his head, he could see Dent Head viaduct and the moor beyond. Shouldering his pack, Jason moved on.

His intention was to head over Blea Moor then drop down to Ribblehead in time to catch the train back. It was a four-hour walk and as he descended to the Hawes road south of the station he checked his watch. He wouldn't have long to wait.

Jason paused at the side of the road to let an old Ford Fiesta past. Surprised when it stopped and reversed back, he bent his head to the driver's window. Lyza looked up at him. "Want a lift?"

Just for a moment Jason hesitated. Then he nodded and climbed in. "Thanks."

"Home?" she said.

"If you're going that way."

She put the car into gear.

Jason threw his pack on the back seat. "I didn't expect to see you so soon?"

"Nan lives in Ingleton. I go over every Wednesday." She glanced across. "Good walk?"

Jason nodded. "No one for miles and completely alone. Could have been the last man on earth." He saw her puzzled face and shrugged. "That's what it felt like anyway."

"You like that? Being completely alone I mean?"

"It's – useful at times."

"Useful?"

"Sometimes I like the isolation."

"But not always?"

Jason smiled. "No. Not always."

"And now?"

"Happy to go back to my little holiday let. Just a number on the face of the earth."

"You're deep."

"I don't mean to be." Jason shook his head. "Just trying to make sense of the world."

Lyza nodded. "Aren't we all?"

The road twisted and turned before it began its ascent to the station. At the top of the rise, Lyza pulled into the little car park and waited while Jason retrieved his pack. He waited a moment, unsure of himself. Surely it wouldn't hurt. Not just once. "Want to come in?" Lyza smiled and turned off the engine. It was all the invite she needed.

She sat at the kitchen table while Jason swilled boiled water around the pot and made tea. He poured it into two china cups then put the kettle back on the hob. Steam misted the air as he sat down. She lifted the cup to her lips. "I can't remember the last time I had real tea."

"Mum used to say, if you're going to do something, do it properly."

"Used to?"

Jason shrugged. "She's gone now."

"Sorry."

"She was old."

Lyza nodded then took another sip. "You've got funny eyes."

"Yeah?"

"Yesterday I swore they were blue."

"Now?"

"They're green. Sort of."

"They change colour."

"To match your moods?"

Jason tipped his head. "That's what Mum always said."

"You must miss her?"

He nodded. "Sometimes."

Lyza put the cup back on the saucer. For a moment they were silent. She picked up a teaspoon and began to bounce it on the rim of her cup. "Is it true?"

"Is what true?"

She paused and put the spoon down. "That your wife was killed?"

The stab went straight to his heart. More so because he never saw it coming.

Jason swallowed and looked at Lyza. "We weren't married," he said. "But yes, Hannah died." Lyza didn't move. "How did you know?"

"Someone in the village said. They remembered your name or face from the papers."

Jason nodded and went to stand by the window. There was always someone. He turned to face her. "We were living in London – an apartment in Shoreditch. She was hit by a train near Blackheath."

"A train? You mean she..."

Jason shook his head. "I don't know. I don't want to know."

"Sorry."

"So am I."

"I mean, I should have thought before asking."

"You would have heard soon enough. Someone always wants to know."

Her eyes widened. "I..."

Jason held up a hand. "I'm glad it was you."

Lyza frowned. "Why?"

"Perhaps, because you're not such a stranger."

For a moment they stared into each other's eyes. Eventually Lyza dropped her gaze and picked up her tea. "Why did you come here?"

"London was too intense. Everyone in my face, telling me how sorry they were then wanting to know the sordid details." Lyza nodded but Jason doubted she understood. How could he explain the emptiness, the hollowness and guilt? How could he explain the mornings when he woke and sleep had snatched the truth from his memory? How could he explain the soul-destroying moment when it flooded back and engulfed him in pain? How? He placed his hands on the draining board and looked out of the window. Dark and melancholy shadows were settling on the hills. "I happened to see this place advertised in one of the Sunday papers. It seemed as good a place as any." He looked back at her and smiled. "And it comes with a view."

"That's about all it's got."

"Don't knock it Lyza. It's pretty special."

"You're just passing through. Things can get," she waved

her hand, "intense here too."

Jason frowned.

"Look, it's like this," she said. "Every minute of every day someone knows where

I am and what I'm doing." She raised her brows. "And who I'm doing it with." She shook her head. "And it'll be like that forever unless..."

"Unless?"

"I get out." She held Jason's eyes.

Jason looked away. "There's a lot to be said for community; friends, family, that sort of thing."

"You think?"

He didn't answer. Friends, family were concepts that had largely passed him by.

For a while they remained in silence. Outside the dusk gathered. Eventually Lyza pushed back her chair. "I have to go," she said and picked her bag off the table. She paused by the door. "There's music in the George, on Friday."

Jason shook his head. "Don't think I'm ready for that."

She stepped away then turned to look back. "I'll be there."

Jason watched her walk to the car, watched the swing of hips, and fall of hair as it bounced on her shoulders. Something gnawed at his insides. It excited him, it frightened him. Jason knew he shouldn't go. But come Friday, he knew he would be there.

*

The band was a three-piece, two boys playing guitars and a girl singer. They set up beneath the TV and, as Jason entered, the pleasant sound of country rock drifted through The George and Dragon's lounge. A few people sat at the tables, tapped their fingers in time to the beat. But most gathered at the bar.

Waiting until a space opened in front of him, Jason slid through the bodies and looked over the counter. A knot of frustration twisted his guts. Lyza wasn't there. Instead it was the landlord, a bull of a man with tattoos on his forearms, who took his order. As he began to pull Jason's pint, he twisted his head to look at the cellar door. "Lyza – Lyza." Muttering beneath his breath, he ran a hand through the sparse strands of his grey hair.

A moment later she emerged from the opening carrying a crate of bottled lager.

The big man's face soured. "Put that down and get on, will yer?" He took his hand off the beer pump and waved it in the air. "People are waiting, Lyza, waiting to be served." Turning back to finish pouring Jason's beer, he shook his head as if the girl were stupid and should know better.

Lyza grimaced and dumped the crate by the fridge door. Hands on hips she looked at the bar scrum, saw Jason, and her face brightened. Ignoring the glasses waved in her face, she went over. "You came?"

"Couldn't resist." A stray elbow jabbed him in the ribs and he jerked forwards.

She laughed. "Drink?"

"Sorted, thanks." Jason motioned with his hand to the big man. He was coming over with his beer. He pushed Lyza out of the way and placed the glass in front of him.

"Well get on, girl."

She slipped aside and mouthed "See you later". Already she was pouring from one of the pumps and taking orders for the next. Still talking, she eyed him across the bar and smiled. Much to his surprise, Jason smiled back.

The night wore on. Though they had little opportunity to talk, Lyza made sure it was she who served him and Jason found himself holding back, hanging on to his glass until she was near and could take his order. Sometime during the evening, he found he was actually enjoying himself.

When the band took a break, and seeing that Lyza was still tied up at the bar,

Jason went outside for a cigarette. A cold wind blew off the fells, so he turned the corner, and found shelter in the lee of the wall. He had just lit up when the door opened and a woman came out. She was round and soft but her eyes were keen, and Jason had the impression she wasn't there just to smoke. Feeling the chill, she pulled her cardigan a little tighter. "Have you got a light, love?"

Jason struck a flame, shielded it with his free hand, and held it across. She inhaled then let the smoke go in a long, satisfied stream. "Needed that," she said and greedily sucked again. "Last of the lepers, we are," she said, and to Jason's puzzled look, gestured with her cigarette. "Unclean to pleasant society."

He nodded understanding.

For a while they shared the silence but Jason guessed there was more. Soon it came. "You the fella who's taken the station house?"

"That's me."

"D'you like it?"

He shuffled inside his jacket. "Yes," he said. "I do."

"Knew a fella once who liked being on his own. Couldn't stand to be in the same room as other people."

"What happened?"

"I divorced him."

Jason grinned.

She held out her hand, "Moira."

Jason quickly took it. As he pulled away, Moira's grip tightened and she stared into his eyes as if she were searching for something. A hint, perhaps, of what lay beneath. He tried again and Moira released his hand.

Jason coughed. "Thanks."

"What for?"

"For being friendly. It's not easy when you're new in town."

"But you've made friends here already, haven't you?"

Puzzled, Jason shook his head. "Have I?"

Moira made a gesture to the pub with her cigarette. "Lisa."

"D'you mean Lyza?"

Moira chuckled. "Lisa by birth. Lyza," and she drew the name out, "by what she answers to." Moira laid a hand on Jason's wrist. "She likes to be a bit different, does Lisa."

"I see."

Moira took a final drag of her cigarette and dropped it on the pavement. "But she's a good kid, is our Lisa." She looked at Jason. She looked hard so there would be no mistake in her words. "We're close here, lad. People look out for one another." She ground the butt beneath her heel. "We wouldn't want to see her get hurt."

There was a moment of silence as they looked into each other's eyes. Jason looked away first. "Me neither," he said.

Moira nodded and wriggled inside her cardigan. "Second half will be starting soon."

Jason showed her the end of his cigarette. "Think I'll finish this first."

"Okay, love." Moira shuffled towards the door. "See you later then."

Jason watched her go then threw the cigarette in the gutter. A bad taste lingered.

He hesitated then took another from the pack. He was just lighting up when Lyza stuck her head around the corner. "So this is where you're hiding."

"Looks that way."

She took the cigarette from his hand and put it between her lips.

"Didn't know you smoked."

Lyza shrugged. "There's a lot about me you don't know." She drew heavily, savoured the taste and exhaled the smoke expertly through her nose. "What did Moira want?"

"Warn me, I guess."

"Warn you?"

"To keep away from you."

Lyza's face darkened. "Fucking cow." She looked at the door and the ghost of

Moira's presence. "Got fuck all to do with her what I do." She took a step as if to follow her inside but Jason shot out a hand and grabbed her wrist.

"It's not a problem."

"It is. Someone's always sticking their nose in. I'm sick of it."

It took a moment for her anger to subside. When it did, Jason found she had moved inside his space. Her body touched his. A pulse, a spark, almost electrical, jolted his insides, and he stepped away from her as if he had been stung. "Lyza," he said. "It's not going to happen."

"Not?"

"No."

"Never?"

He closed his eyes. "I can't."

"Can't or won't?"

Jason said nothing. How could he make her understand? He took a deep breath, but just as he opened his mouth the landlord appeared.

"Christ, Lyza, how long you going to be?" He made an

attempt to grab her wrist but she shrank behind Jason, and he was left snatching air. Behind, and looking over his shoulder, was Wayne. In an effort to maintain his dignity, the landlord beckoned Lyza inside. "C'mon," he said. "Move it." He hesitated, wondered if he should say more, then turned and disappeared back to his domain.

Wayne stayed. His eyes roved from Lyza to Jason then back again. "What're you doing? Out here with him."

"Talking," she said and held up the stub of her cigarette. "And finishing this."

His eyes narrowed. "You don't smoke."

"Give us a break, Wayne. I do what I like."

Wayne jerked his chin at Jason. "Not with him."

Lyza looked at the floor then at Jason. "What did I tell you?"

Wayne's eyes darted back to Lyza. "Tell him? Tell him what?"

Lyza said nothing. She held up her hand and let the butt fall through her fingers.

Pushing past Wayne she paused on the step and looked back. "See you later?"

Jason shrugged. "Maybe." He waited for Wayne to say something but after puffing out his chest and giving him his best dead-eye look, he followed Lyza inside.

For a little while Jason stood looking at the open door. Beyond lay laughter, music, an escape from loneliness. Then he looked towards the empty moors and remembered why he was there. Jason sighed, turned his back on the lights, and began to walk home.

*

Jason walked quickly. Dark hills loomed on every side. As the road began to climb he increased his pace in an effort to speed his journey. The road was empty, the air still, and the George's warmth and comfort a long way behind when he heard a boot scuff the tarmac. He stopped, and as he began to turn, a fist caught his cheek. Jason went sprawling. Spreading his arms to cushion the fall, he landed heavily. Sharp gravel tore into his palms. He stifled a yell before a kick in his kidneys sent him tumbling onto his back. Before he knew what was happening

86

Wayne was on him, hand around his throat, and knee in his groin.

Jason reached out, tried to hold him off, but he had no air, could scarcely breathe, and Wayne was strong. He knocked his arms away and rained down punch after punch. In the end he shielded his body and took the blows as best he could.

Eventually Wayne stopped. He was panting, had exhausted himself on the beating, and wearily climbed off Jason. A moment passed, then he bent close to Jason's face. "We don't want you see. Don't want you here." Grabbing the collar on Jason's jacket, he pulled him forward so they were only inches apart and Jason could smell the sour beer-mash on his breath. "You keep to your sen, and we'll keep to ours." He thrust Jason's head back – back so hard, it thudded on the tarmac. "And leave our lass be."

A light exploded in Jason's brain. He heard a distant voice cry out but had no idea whether it was his own or someone else's. Nor did he know how long he lay at the side of the road. But when his vision cleared, and life returned, he was quite alone.

Jason stirred, rolled onto his stomach, and pushed himself to his knees. He probed his ribs. A wave of nausea rose as he found the last point of contact. Getting to his feet, he looked himself over. His hands were cut and ribs sore, there was blood in his mouth, and his clothes were torn. He shook his head. "What the fuck am I doing?" He set off, staggering towards the station house a mile distant, feeling the pain with every step. And as he walked he almost laughed. He hadn't yet been there a week.

*

Next day Jason stayed inside. A hot-water bath made the pain easier. There was no TV, radio reception was poor and the book he was trying to read made little sense. He flung it in a corner and spent most of the day staring through the window.

He heard the car long before it came into sight. Growling as it climbed the road from the village, it stopped outside. He knew it was her before she even rapped on the door. For a moment neither moved. Then Lyza lifted a hand and traced the contours of his bruised face. Before he knew it, she was pushing him back, pressing her body close until the wall halted his retreat, and he could go no further. He smelled her hair, her skin – her odour filled his senses. Jason couldn't help himself. He cupped her face in his hands and found her lips. Pure and sweet, for a moment he was lost. Then a frozen image flashed into his mind: Hannah's corpse face as he made the ID at Greenwich mortuary.

Jason gagged, pushed her away, and turned his face to the wall. Bile and the sour taste of death turned his stomach. Lyza said nothing. She waited and watched and when he finally faced her, she just stood there. Was it triumph or pity he saw in her eyes? He wiped his mouth with the back of his hand. "Thought you had a boyfriend."

She ran a hand over her breasts, smoothing her top. "What if I do?"

Jason shook his head. He had nothing to say.

Lyza stepped back and looked Jason over. Her eyes creased in concern. "I heard what happened."

Jason jerked a shoulder. It didn't matter.

"He's a prick," said Lyza.

"Well you should know."

They held each other's eyes. A moment later they both laughed. Jason grimaced and pushed his tongue into his cheek. "Shouldn't have done that."

"You mean it only hurts when you laugh?"

Jason looked at Lyza. He reached out to touch her face then dropped his hand.

"You shouldn't be here."

"No?"

"All I want is a quiet life."

"And?"

"And you complicate things."

She smirked and turned her back on him. Before she stepped through the door, she stopped and turned her head. "I will make you love me."

Jason watched her walk to the car and drive away. And with each beat of his heart, each intake of breath, his fear grew. He clenched his fists. Maybe this time would be different. He closed the door and rested his head against the wood. With sudden fury, he beat the flat of his hand against the panel. "No, no, no." He wouldn't let it happen. Blood seeped through the bandage on his hand. Lyza was eating his self-control.

Jason wandered to the kitchen, made tea and stared at the walls. He couldn't sit still. There was too much going on in his head. Eventually he put on his coat and ventured onto the moors.

As he started the ascent of Knoutberry Hill, the rain began. Cold drops flew into his face and he looked skywards the better to feel its beat. It was an exercise in self-abasement, a scouring of the soul, and as he walked he began to murmur "Sorry Hannah, sorry Hannah" over and over until his throat was sore and mind numb. But it was Lyza who stained his soul with her memory. Jumping a dry-stone wall, a crow took flight. For a instant it hovered over a sheep's ragged carcass, then feeling the wind beneath its wings, followed Jason to the summit.

Jason stared across the void. Winter was coming. He felt it in the air, felt it in his bones. Far away a column of cloud bled towards him. It was low and encased the world in a grey shroud. High above, his black companion sailed effortlessly on. Jason watched, cupping a hand over his eyes, until it was nothing more than a black speck in the distance. How easy would it be to follow the wind, lose oneself and never turn back? For a moment Jason was lost in speculation. Then with the inevitability of his existence, he turned for home.

Lyza was waiting. Standing by the open car door she watched him approach. She had rouged her cheeks and darkened her eyes; she wore a short skirt and long boots. She looked like a whore. Jason took her hand and gazed into her eyes. Then he led her inside.

Jason immersed himself in her body: her arms, her belly, the soft white of her breasts. He suckled and kneaded, pounded and caressed – their clothes lay in heaps upon the floor. Never before had he given himself so fully to another. Not even Hannah. Lyza's secret scents and Jason's musk mingled, sweat and sweet salt tears combined as they tore into each other, more animal than human. And at the end, when they had given and received in equal measure, they climaxed, and screamed into the night. Later, smelling of sex, their bodies moist, they lay atop the bed and shared a cigarette.

Lyza took it from Jason's lips and placed it in her own. A stream of smoke escaped her mouth. "How long you going to be around?"

Jason watched the lazy trail of smoke curl to the ceiling. "What's that?"

"I'm guessing you won't be around forever."

"I guess not."

Lyza wriggled out of his arms. "I'm serious," she said. "A week, a month?"

Jason struggled up into a sitting position. "I don't know."

She frowned at him.

"Really I don't. I've taken the cottage on a three-month lease. After that –" He pulled a face. "I guess I'll move on."

Satisfied with his answer, she pushed him back and lay her head on his chest.

"Good," she said. "When you go, take me with you."

*

Just before midnight, Lyza dressed, kissed Jason goodbye and slipped back to the village.

Jason slept. He had entered a state of peace, a safe place where his fears lay submerged beneath the memory of Lyza's sweet body. But something niggled. Something vague and black, and when he thought on it later, utterly predictable. Through the depth of dream, through a layer of unconscious thought, it came unbidden. And it came to him as a voice, a woman's voice – Hannah's voice. So close was she that Jason felt the wisp of breath on his ear. And she whispered just three words: "Always and forever."

Jason woke.

She was back. Just as she always came back. In the heartbeat it took to emerge from sleep, he scanned the room; corner to corner, floor to ceiling. It was empty. No phantom lurked in the shadows. Jason's racing heart slowed and he closed his eyes. Maybe it was a dream. Maybe. But even as he said it, he knew it for a lie. For wasn't that what he always said? This time he thought it might be different. But no. She had found him again. Pricked by cold, consumed by fear, he threw the covers aside and got out of bed. He sniffed the air. Something lingered, something that shouldn't be there. He went to the hall and opened the door.

The station lights were extinguished and it was dark. A dark so complete, rarely does it touch the sight of man. The moon hung low in the sky. Clouds scudded past, outriders for the storm Jason felt sure was coming, and he looked left and right, up and down seeking some hint as to what form that storm would take.

He saw nothing but an old dog fox stepping across the tracks. It paused in its journey and set sad eyes upon him. Then it continued on its way as if he were not there at all. Jason shivered. He went back, locked the door, and returned to bed. But he did not sleep. Only when dawn's grey light filtered through his window did he fall into uneasy slumber. And he slept with a woman on his mind and her perfume in the air. It was a scent he knew well. And it wasn't Lyza's.

*

The morning wasn't easy. Jason sat in the kitchen while Hannah and Lyza slipped in and out of his head. One flushed him with guilt, the other with excitement. Breakfast stuck in his throat. He had to see her.

An hour later he was standing in the rain-locked street outside the George. It was that curious time in a pub's life, open but empty of customers. Jason checked each room before walking into the lounge. He didn't even know if she was working. Footsteps made him turn.

Moira stared at him. "You've got a nerve," she said and jabbed the mop in her hand at him.

Jason stepped back.

"Didn't think you had it in you," she said. "There's a dryness about you, a body lacking spirit, and you'll suck the life from anyone fool enough to let them." For a moment she was silent then looked hard into Jason's eyes. He dropped his gaze. Moira moved closer and her voice softened. "You don't belong here, lad." She shrugged. "I'm not sure you belong anywhere." She reached out to touch his arm and there was tenderness, almost a sadness in her actions. "Why don't you leave our Lisa be? She's happy here. She may not know or appreciate it – but she is. Go on, lad," and she nudged him with her elbow. "You know no good will come of it. Why don't you..."

"Why doesn't he do what?" Lyza stood by the door, and stared down Moira. "My dad pays you to clean the floors – not for giving advice."

Moira's face soured. "I've said my piece."

"Yes you have," said Lyza. "Have you done the toilets?"

"No. I was just..."

Lyza cocked an eyebrow.

Moira sniffed and shuffled out. Lyza watched her go then turned to look at Jason.

"What're you doing here?"

"I wanted – needed to see you."

Lyza said nothing.

Jason opened his arms then flapped them helplessly at his side. "I've been thinking about you." The words he needed weren't there and with little encouragement from Lyza, he began to stammer. Then a thought struck and his stomach tightened. "Is Wayne here?"

A sly smile teased itself from Lyza's mouth. "Why, d'you want him?"

"No I don't."

She waited a moment then her face lightened. "He won't be in till later. Sunday lunch and all that." She raised her eyes. Muffled voices could be heard through the ceiling. "You shouldn't have come." She motioned her head to the door and stairs beyond. "Moira's gone to tell Dad."

"Dad?"

"You met him the other night. He's pissed that I missed my shift last night."

"You live here?"

"Yeah, and he blames you." She led him to the door and almost pushed him out.

Jason stood on the step, reluctant to leave. Lyza glanced over her shoulder then flicked a hand. "Go."

"Will I see you tonight?"

Slowly she smiled. "Yeah," she said, "you will." She kissed him, turned her back and went inside. Jason checked his watch and counted the hours. It was going to be a long day.

*

Jason waited. He sat in the kitchen and waited while the hands of the clock slowly turned. He waited as the last passenger boarded the last train; and he waited as day gave way to night, and a brittle moon reared its head over Dentdale moor. When at last he heard her car and bare-knuckle rap on the door, he could wait no more.

They fucked in the hall.

Clothes torn and pulled apart, he held her shoulders against the wall and pushed himself inside her. She bit, kissed then bit again. He tasted blood, felt it run down his cheek but didn't care. She pressed close, wrapped herself around him, responding to his thrusts until their rhythm became one. He was lost, out of control and the only thing between him and madness was Lyza's body. Only when he looked up and saw a face in the mirror that was not his own did sanity return. His scream was of agony not ecstasy.

Jason took her to the bedroom and tried again. But he was distracted, half-hearted, and Lyza pushed him away. She sat on the edge of the bed, smoking a cigarette. "Were you thinking about her?"

"Hannah?"

She didn't answer.

"I always think about her."

"That's not nice."

His stomach knotted. "Not like that." He crawled across the bed and laid a hand on her shoulder. "Not when we were making love. It's you, only you I think about." She shrugged his hand away but he tried again, gently massaging her neck. "I mean she's up here." He tapped his temple." Lyza turned her face and allowed him to kiss her cheek.

"You have to let her go, Jay."

He nodded. "Sometimes I think it's she who won't let me go."

Lyza held his hand and squeezed. "You need help."

"I need you."

She moved away and began to dress. Jason looked on. "Don't go, Hannah."

Lyza froze. "What?"

"Please don't go."

"You called me Hannah."

Jason closed his eyes. He opened his hands, palms up in a gesture of apology but it was too late.

"Bastard." Her voice rose. "You called me Hannah."

"Sorry" was too small a word but the only thing Jason could think of. He said it again.

Lyza turned away and began to dress. "You have to decide, Jay." She slipped her top over her head and pulled it down. "Do you want to live with her, a memory of the past?" She stepped into her skirt. "Or do you want flesh and blood, something real?" She picked up her coat and walked away. "I won't share you, Jay. Not even with a ghost." She stormed out, the irony lost on her, and slammed the door behind her. A moment later he heard her car screech away.

Jason sat on the bed, smoked a cigarette, and then another. It had begun. And he knew for Lyza and the sake of his sanity, he had to stay strong. In the dark he waited for her to come. Sometime after midnight, she did.

A single, shrill cry punched the night. It was her. He closed his eyes and remembered her cries of despair that last night when he confessed his deceit. That he loved another. And he remembered her screaming that if didn't want her then he would never have another. Hadn't they promised, "always and forever"?

Jason closed his eyes. If he could take it back, change things, would he? Too late.

Much too late.

Steeling himself, he padded across the floor and listened at the kitchen door. Still her cries flowed on the other side. Pushing it open, he reached for the light. The sound ceased. A moment later they returned, elsewhere, and Jason followed her sobbing until he had searched every room, every space and hidden corner until he stood by the door in the hall. He flung it back.

Outside, it was cold and still. On the bank above the track, railway sleepers stood like gravestones in a cemetery gone to ruin. Jason shivered. His breaths came in short rapid bursts. He walked the platform edge, past the row of darkened lamps, to the very end. Moon-shadows stalked him as he looked into the void that was night.

She was there, just as he knew she would be there. But no vision of beauty this, no memory of desire did she conjure in Jason – for she bore the mark of the grave. Her red hair was faded and matted, her features corrupted by decay, and her skin – that skin she worshipped at the altar of vanity, the skin she oiled and massaged every night – was brown and paper thin.

The cold earth had left only a desperate, hollow shell.

His convictions vanished. His sanity, his soul, demanded he stay strong and deny her. But he was weak, had always been weak. Only with her was he complete. There was no escape. She turned her tortured eyes upon him and beckoned him to her.

And just like he always used to, Jason went. One step and then another. No longer in control, foot followed foot.

A deep roar burst the night. The spell broken, Jason gasped and flung himself away from the edge. He fell hard. The cold stone tore the breath from his body. Crumpled on the floor, Jason looked. A coal-laden train rumbled past. As the engine cleared the southbound platform, the driver gave it its head. Engines throbbed, exhausts belched, and down she went. Down towards Arten Gill and Ribblehead, down towards Settle and Leeds – down towards Hannah standing in its way.

Jason watched. He screamed, called her name but it was lost in the noise of the wagons rolling by. Turning away, he buried his head in his arms and sobbed. He stayed like that long after it was gone. Eventually, as silence sealed the night once more, he raised his head. But of Hannah – there was nothing.

*

For three days Jason locked himself away. He smoked, stared at the wall and waited for night to come. For the nights were the worst. She invaded his dreams, tormented his soul, cried in the dark until he could stand no more, and he stood beside the track wanting to hurl himself beneath the wheels of the next iron monster and end it for good. And every night the same thing happened. His resolve weakened and he turned aside, seeking the false comfort of his bed.

It was noon on the fourth day when he heard her car.

"Christ, you look awful." Lyza pushed past him into the kitchen. She put a bag of groceries on the table. "You just got up?"

Jason rubbed his chin. "Yeah – no." He shook his head. "Not been sleeping well is all." Self-consciously, he twisted the belt of his dressing gown tighter. Unable to meet her eyes, he wandered to the sink and began to search the drawers. Finding an open pack of cigarettes he flipped the lid. There were two left. He took one and passed the other to Lyza. She watched him fumble with the lighter then took it from him. She lit it herself. There was an awkward silence.

"Lyza," he began. "The other night. I'm sorry."

"Are you?"

"Yes."

She nodded. "D'you know what it is you want, Jay."

"I know now," he said. "I thought I could fight it but..."

"There's nothing to fight, Jay. You do what you want to do."

"Or have to," he said.

She shook her head. "You don't have to do anything."

He smiled sadly. She wouldn't understand.

Lyza shrugged. "Well?"

He moved closer, put his hands on her shoulders and gazed into her eyes. "I want us to be together."

"For always?"

"Yes."

"Say it."

He looked at Lyza, looked into her face and remembered another time and another girl but the same promise. But it didn't matter. "Always," he said. "Always and forever."

Lyza sighed. It was a sigh of triumph. "Let's go somewhere."

"When?"

She stubbed the cigarette into an ashtray. "Tomorrow. I'll pick you up. We can make plans."

Jason followed her to the door. "Sure," he said and smiled as she pecked him on the cheek.

"Tomorrow then?"

He nodded, watched her climb into her car and closed the door behind her. Going into the lounge, he sank into an armchair and closed his eyes. A minute passed before a knock on the door roused him. Thinking she was back, he walked through the hall and pulled it open. "Can't keep away..."

Wayne filled the doorway. For a few seconds they looked each other in the eye.

Then Wayne's hand shot out and caught Jason around the throat. He pushed forward, forcing Jason back until he crashed into the wall. Pain sliced into his shoulders. He grasped Wayne's wrist trying to loosen his hold but Wayne was too strong, and used his weight to pin him back. He said nothing but his red-rimmed eyes spoke pure hatred. As his grip tightened, black spots appeared before Jason's eyes. He was losing consciousness. Felt himself going down to a place rarely visited. But it was a place he knew well. Finally, he gave in.

Holding himself rigid, Jason pushed off the wall with his foot and lowered his head. At the same time he turned the hand holding his throat. Jason's head jerked forward and caught Wayne on the bridge of his nose. Something cracked. As Wayne cried out his grip loosened and Jason brought his knee into his groin. Wayne doubled over. As he bent forward he used his knee again, this time in his face. Wayne went down.

And that's where it should have ended. But it didn't.

Something inside Jason was broken and he looked at his adversary without pity or remorse. As Wayne crawled for the door, Jason kicked then kicked again. He was an insect to be humiliated and squashed. Wayne rolled into a foetal position and used his arms and hands to protect face and body. It did little good. Jason stamped down until flesh grew soft and bones ground beneath his heel. He felt nothing. Only when he looked up and saw his wild face in the mirror, did he relent. Wayne was hardly moving.

Jason grabbed his collar and pulled him across the floor to the door. As the cold air reached his lungs Wayne gasped. Jason took a huge breath, bent down and heaved Wayne to his feet. One arm around his shoulders, Jason half carried and half dragged him to his car. He opened the door, pushed him across the driver's seat, and slammed it shut. Jason went back. He made coffee, settled back in his chair and started reading. It was a good book and he didn't stop till midnight. And when he went to bed, he slept soundly. No dreams, no cries in the night – nothing but sweet oblivion. It was all he ever wanted.

*

They drove to Leeds. Lyza loved the urban environment. She swathed herself in the anonymity of a big city, lost herself in the shops and malls. On the way back they stopped in Settle, drank wine, and made love in the back seat of the car. When they drew up outside the George, it was almost closing time.

A dozen pairs of eyes followed as they walked into the lounge. Glasses paused halfway to lips, chatter ceased. Someone strangled a laugh.

Lyza scanned the faces. "What?"

Sitting on a stool at the bar, an empty wineglass in front of her, Moira just shook her head. "What d'you want to bring him here for?"

"Why shouldn't I?"

"After what he done to Wayne too."

Lyza checked herself. "Why, what's happened to Wayne?"

"Lad's in hospital, that's what." She tipped her head in Jason's direction. "And he put him there."

Lyza turned her head to look at Jason. She squeezed his wrist. "Tell me."

Jason sighed. "Yesterday, he must have followed you to my place. When I opened the door he was standing on the step." Jason shrugged. "I just defended myself."

The silence deepened. Lyza stared into Jason's eyes. Just for a moment he thought it wasn't going to happen. Then she put her arms around his neck and drew him close. As she kissed him, a collective groan echoed around the pub but Jason didn't care. It was too late.

As she released him Lyza whispered, "Wait for me outside."

Jason shook his head. "I'm fine here."

"Please." She handed him the car keys.

Jason relented. He looked at the people around the bar, searched their faces one by one. When he reached Moira, he paused and held her gaze until she looked away. Then he went to wait by the car.

He was leaning on the bonnet smoking a cigarette when Lyza emerged carrying a small suitcase. Jason took it and threw it on the back seat of the car. They kissed. For a moment they stood looking at one another, unsure what to do next.

Lyza hugged him. "Told you I'd make you love me."

"Yes you did." Jason nodded. He had tried but it wasn't enough. He had promised

Hannah "Always and forever" and she kept him to his word. She wouldn't let him go – not now, not ever.

Lyza held out her hand for the keys but Jason closed his fist around them. "I'll drive," he said.

"Where to?"

"Just a place I know." He looked up at the stars. "I go there sometimes. When I need to find some peace."

"If it's away from here then I like it," she said, and pecked him on the cheek. He watched her forehead wrinkle. "Your eyes," she said, "they've changed colour again. They're very dark tonight."

"Yes," he said and opened the door for her to climb in. "I guess they are."

Deadbait

From the balcony of my apartment, I watched the Boy – different day, same routine. He was walking between the bars and restaurants lining the Avenida del Carmen and making his way towards the sea: rod in one hand, bait-bag in the other. Halting by the jetty, he scanned the water before slipping between the harbour wall and the narrow inlet that flowed beneath the cliffs. At that point he was lost to sight but three hours later I knew he would emerge and make the same journey in reverse.

I had given myself six days: three to observe, one to set up and one to act. The last kept in reserve for tying up loose ends. Today I was setting things in motion. I waited two hours then went down.

"Caught much?"

My sudden appearance startled him. He turned wondering how I had negotiated the rocks without hearing me. He squinted, trying to decide whether I was someone of his father's acquaintance or someone important enough that he should acknowledge my presence. Deciding I was neither he shook his blond head and turned back to the water and the bright-red float bobbing fifteen metres out. He was a good-looking kid: twelve – thirteen in a few weeks, with a wide-eyed expression that seemed to question all he saw. There was a flush of pink on his pale cheeks and something in his eyes and nose that was familiar. I sniffed. Sometimes I hate loose ends.

Feeling I was still there, he half-turned, frowned, and at that moment I think he had a bad feeling that maybe I represented some kind of threat. I did my best, smiled and squatted, taking myself down to the same height as himself. But these days what kid doesn't see a bogeyman in every adult that says hello? Already the morning sun beat against the harbour wall. It was going to be a hot one.

I jerked my head in the direction of his line. "What bait are you using?"

He continued to stare at me, the way a kid does; eschewing the inhibitions controlling so much of our lives until he was satisfied it was safe to answer. He gestured to the plastic bag at his feet. "Squid."

"Frozen?"

He nodded.

"Not much joy?"

"Nope."

I pursed my lips in a way that suggested I was mulling over his difficulties.

"Here," I said, "try this." Peeved that I should interfere yet intrigued by the possibility I knew more than he, his brow furrowed. But a fisherman without fish would take advice from the devil if it meant he went home with a full catch. I opened the paper bag in my hand and tore a piece of crust from the loaf I'd just bought from the Mercado. I handed it over. He wrinkled his nose as if it smelt then looked at me as if I were mad and my fishing expertise illusory. The raising of hope was dashed.

"Bread?" he said.

"Sure. Watch this," and I tore off another piece and tossed it into the water. It floated for a few seconds before a swirl of water marked a passing fish's interest. The boy saw it and stood perfectly still. Within a few seconds a flash of rising silver marked its return. It snatched at the bread and with a flick of its tail disappeared. The boy was transfixed. He watched the water, watched the circle of ripples contract around the remnant of bread still floating on the tide, and as he turned his face to me, another fish rose and finished what was left on the surface. He heard the splash and just saw the bread disappear into its hungry maw.

"Wow!"

His face was alive. I smiled, remembering the way it was – the way I felt as a boy trying to tempt a trout from the stream with nothing more than my grandfather's old cane rod and a worm dug from the garden. I spent hours on the bank. And every rise would turn my mouth to dust and set my heart hammering against the wall of my chest. I could see the boy felt the same.

He looked at the bread in his hand as if it were a concoction of wonder. He wasted no time. Placing the bread in his pocked, he reeled in his line, tore off the strip of squid and replaced it on the hook with a thumbnail-size piece of bread. As he cast in, he looked back and bit his lip, remembering in his excitement that he'd forgotten to thank me, then concentrated on his float. The float drifted, the line bowed and I watched the boy expertly keeping control until without warning the float disappeared. The boy struck. He lifted the rod and wound down quickly only to find the fish had taken the bait and avoided the barb with as much skill as the boy was showing in his fishing. Slowly he brought the line back to the shore.

Just for a moment he paused. He frowned looking at the empty hook and the place where he felt sure a fish should have been. He shrugged, broke another bread flake from the piece I'd given him and pushed it on the hook. With a flick of his wrist, he sent bait and float skittering onto the water. He glanced back and raised his brows. I nodded encouragement. This time.

Within seconds a pale dorsal fin cut the water near his line and as his float bobbed under, the boy struck – harder this time, but with the same result. He groaned aloud and looked over his shoulder. "That was a big one."

We were mates now and I smiled back. "Plenty more," I said.

He nodded, encouraged by the thought that there was an endless supply of fish just waiting to throw themselves at his bait. All he had to do was hook one – just one.

He recast, set the bail arm on his reel and waited. A small shoal began to gather offshore and as soon as the bait hit the water they were on to it. The boy missed again and this time he slapped a hand to his forehead wondering what it was he was doing wrong. Frustrated, he reeled in. Just before he put another piece of bread on the hook, he looked back at me, wondering if he should ask, wondering if I had the answers to the mysteries of the deep.

It was time.

"How are you putting the bread on?"

"Like this," he said and held up hands showing me how he pushed the point of the hook through the bread.

I rubbed my chin. "Thing is," I said. "It won't stay on like that."

His brows wrinkled.

I scrambled down to where he was standing. "Can I show you?"

He looked up at me, his blue eyes searching my face and, seeing nothing more than a fisherman passing on his knowledge, handed the rod to me.

"It's like this," I said. "These fish are clever. The water's so clear that they can see the hook in the bread," and I held up the line, hook and bread suspended as if it were in the water. "They snatch at the corner and suck it off the hook." I mimicked a fish's mouth with my hand and pulled the bread from the hook. "Unless you're lucky, they'll never touch the barb." The boy nodded. "You have to set the bait so that they come back, and then back again until they're convinced if they don't grab it, another fish will."

"But you said the bread will tear off?"

I raised my brows and smiled. "There's a trick. Want me to show you?"

"Yeah."

"Pass me your knife."

He reached into his back pocket and pulled out a wooden-handled clasp knife.

It was almost new. I read the Opinal logo and turned it over in my hand. "You been to France?"

No doubt encouraged by his father, the boy's face clouded with a studied wariness. He shrugged and I let the matter drop. Apart from professional pride, it didn't matter now anyhow.

I opened the knife and cut the hook from the line. "Like this," I said and crouched down so he could see what I was doing. I put the hook in my hand, looped the line through it and made a circle. Winding the line several times along its own length, I threaded it back and knotted it above the hook's shank. The boy looked puzzled.

"Pass me the bread." He did and I took a piece, placed it into the centre of the line and pulled. Like a noose the line closed over it and the hook disappeared inside the bread. "There," I said. "That will stay on."

The boy looked at me as if I'd passed on the secrets of the universe. He took the rod, opened the reel's bail-arm and cast it into the sea. Almost immediately the float bobbed. He lifted the rod before it settled again.

"Wait," I said and lifted a hand. "Wait until it disappears."

Again it moved. It lay horizontal to the water before it returned to an upright position. I opened my mouth to warn but didn't have to, the boy had discipline and learnt quickly. And then it went. The float streamed away, its red spot a beacon beneath the surface, and before I could say the word, the boy had flicked the rod up and reeled down hard. It was on, a good fish by the bend in the rod. The boy bounced from foot to foot as he felt its power surge through the rod tip.

"The drag," I said. "Set the drag."

My words cut through his excitement and he eased it a half-turn back and began to reel in.

"Not too fast," I said. "The hook might pull out."

He nodded, all the time watching the water and line. Using the rod's length, he steered the fish. As it neared, it broke the surface and I heard him gasp. Sunlight caught its flank and for the first time, revealed its size. But it had seen the shore now, seen the rock where the boy stood, and understood its danger. It turned and powered away. Line fled from the boy's reel, the ratchet cranking as once more it went deep.

"Keep it tight," and I moved my hand and arm up as if I were holding an imaginary rod. I was sweating, my heart pounding, and I realised that I had gotten involved in the boy's excitement. "Bring him in close," I said and moved down to the water's edge. As the boy brought the fish in, I reached out, took the line and moved my hand down until I could feel the fish's belly.

"Don't lose it," said the boy. "Don't lose it now."

Two fingers inside the gill and I lifted it clear of the water.

The boy almost dropped the rod and ran to take it in both hands. From the look on his face it was Christmas and his birthday all rolled into one.

"That's a nice fish."

We both turned our heads. Standing on the harbour wall, a man was watching.

How long he had been there I didn't know but he had a slight, amused smile on his lips and I figured he had been there a while.

The boy hesitated before his excitement got the better of him. He held up the fish. "Look at this, Dad."

He nodded, jumped down and clasped a hand on the boy's shoulder. "Well done son." But he wasn't looking at the fish, nor the boy.

He was looking at me.

I put on my best, false smile, wiped a fishy hand on my shirt and held it out.

"Adam Sadler," I said. He was a scrawny guy with a sparse goatee scribbled on his face as if by a child's crayon. He wore a blue Hawaiian shirt and a pair of khaki shorts that hung off him like they were a size too big. That friendly grin never left his face but behind his eyes there was a deep-seated mistrust of anything out of the ordinary. And that included me.

He waited a moment then with a slight nod, took my hand. "Barry Evans."

I nodded: Barry Evans alias John Curtis, alias Peter Briscoe, alias – well, the closest I got to the name he was given after dropping from his mother's womb was Johnny Gee.

But that was okay because Adam Sadler wasn't my name either.

He had made his name but hardly a fortune ripping off people who didn't have the gumption to do anything about it. Unfortunately for Barry – or Johnny Gee, this time he had ripped off the wrong person.

He dropped my hand and turned his attention to the boy. "That's a good fish son," he said then made a show of glancing at his watch and raising an eyebrow. "But you should have been back an hour ago." There was an accent, a slight nasal whine hinting at Brooklyn or Queen's, that he was trying, but hadn't quite managed, to disguise.

The boy's excitement was caught. "Oh yeah. Sorry." He said it quietly as if the word stuck in his throat. He looked back to the fish, his triumph falling away like sand in an hour glass.

"I've told you, Paul, you have to do as I say. We agreed, didn't we? Why, anything could have happened. Anymore of this and there'll be no more fishing."

Time to play the martyr. I held my hands up in a gesture of apology. "My fault," I said.

"If I'm not fishing, I like to watch someone else." I shrugged. "I saw the boy and came over. Afraid we both got a bit carried away."

Barry said nothing. Not at first. But he cocked his head to one side and eyed me suspiciously. "If you don't mind me saying," he said, "you don't look much like a fisherman."

I jerked a thumb behind me. "My stuff's up at the apartment,

I was taking a walk when I saw your boy fishing."

He nodded at this, seemed vaguely satisfied with my answer, then patted Paul on the shoulder. "C'mon," he said. "Put the fish back and collect you stuff. We have to go."

"Aw, Dad. Do I have too?"

"We do. You've already been here longer than I said you could." Again he looked over at me. "And Mr Sadler must have things to do."

I took the hint. "It was nice meeting you, Paul," I said. "You too, Barry," and I held out my hand again.

He sighed and stretched across. Fed up with my overt friendliness, the shake was perfunctory and he immediately turned away. "C'mon, Paul, get your rod and bag."

I walked back over the rocks. Just before I climbed the breakwater wall and returned to the path, I turned. "Hey, Paul." I held up my hand as if it held a rod. "Tight lines, huh."

He smiled, took his hands from the water where he had just released his fish and waved farewell. But it wasn't. I would be seeing him and his father again very soon.

*

That night I made sure I was in Annabella's before Barry Evans.

Discreet enquiries and late night wanderings revealed a predilection for cheap women and cheaper bars. He was as predictable as the boy and had a routine you could set your watch by. I sat on a stool at the counter, minding my own business and watching the entrance through a mirror behind the bar.

At ten the street outside was buzzing. Laughter and a steady rock rhythm punctuated the night while the free flow of cheap booze made for a heady atmosphere, and a headache for the local cops. Run by Mitch, a Scotsman and rabid Rangers supporter, framed blue shirts, autographed by their previous owners, daubed the walls. Misplaced loyalty that valued the Queen as the true bastion and lasting bulwark against the pope and Catholicism in general manifested itself in a regal portrait behind the bar.

Behind me and sitting at a booth table were three men. They had the pasty-faced hue of the new arrival and the demeanour of the heavy drinker. The one nearest was a big guy, carried some weight and had a thatch of red, almost orange, hair that looked like it had been glued in place. One quick glance told me they neared the limit of intoxication. At a table near the entrance, drinking bottled Magners, were a younger couple. Shorts and sandals, T-shirts and tattoos seemed the accepted mode of dress.

I didn't wait long. Through the mirror I clocked Evans as he stepped over the threshold and into the bar. He paused when he saw me. A moment of indecision as his mind turned over the possibilities of my being there, then he jutted his chin forward and came to stand next to me.

I turned my head and feigned surprise. "Hey, Barry," I said and held out my hand. He said nothing – not at first. But I watched the skin tighten around his eyes. A second, maybe two, passed before he took my hand and squeezed.

"Adam, isn't it?"

I nodded and he sat on the next stool and placed his mobile phone on the counter. I looked at it and then him.

"Expecting a call," he said. "Business."

I ordered him a beer and he took several large swallows before replacing it on the counter. He wiped his mouth with the back of his hand and swivelled his head to look at me. There was a haze in his eyes, a watery film he could do nothing to disguise. If he kept to his usual routine, Annabella's would be the fourth bar on his run. Four bars, four beers. I guessed he hadn't deviated.

"So," he said at last. "How comes your 'ere?"

I shrugged. "Came out for some food." I jerked my thumb back towards the strip of bars and restaurants. "Terraza Playa, just above the beach. Paella's excellent." I picked up my glass. "Washing it down with a beer before I head back."

His face darkened. "I mean here," and he used a finger to jab the counter. "Lanzarote – just you is it? On your own? Don't seem right."

"I'm working. Writing in the morning and..." I pulled a face. "Fishing or," I tried a little laugh, "watching someone else fish later."

"Writing huh?"

"I'm doing a travel piece. What to see, where to go, that sort of thing."

Evans snorted. "You mean the caves or the volcano?"

107

"Yeah," I said and rubbed my neck. "It is a little limited."

"Limited. Rock stuck in the middle of the fucking Atlantic is what it is." He took another swallow of his beer.

"Want another?"

He looked at the remains and nodded. "Yeah, I will." He pushed the glass across and folded his arms on the counter while I caught the barman's eye.

"Have you taken Paul to Timanfaya?"

"Yeah," he said. "It was one of the things he wanted to do." Barry shrugged.

"You know – walk up a one-in-four slope and watch a guy make toast and boil water." He shook his head. "Fuck me, that's what I have a kettle and toaster for." He took a slug of his beer and placed the glass heavily on the counter. He had started to relax, and, off guard, so had his accent – pure New York.

I laughed. "Yeah," I said. "There's not a lot of touristy things. In fact I'm struggling to find an angle."

"Angle?"

I made an open-handed gesture. "A way of putting things. You know – for the article."

"Ah." His face cleared.

"Perhaps I should concentrate on the more mundane: the island's beauty and wildlife."

"Wildlife? Are you for real? A few scrawny lizards and birds that got lost on their way to Africa?"

"Maybe, but the marine life is spectacular." I opened my hands. "I've never seen such a variety of fish." I lifted my glass then stopped halfway to my mouth as if the thought had just occurred. "Hey," I said. "Maybe I could do a story on you and the boy, snorkelling, fishing – take a few pics. The human angle you know?"

He looked at me as if I were mad. "There wouldn't be any pictures."

"No?"

"Believe me – no pictures." And then he did a curious thing. Instead of dismissing my suggestion, he rubbed his chin. "Me and the boy ain't that close." He looked and pulled a face. "I've been away a lot. Had to go at the drop of a hat – you know, foreign travel. Sometimes I never even had time to say goodbye. Work," he said. "It's taken me to some strange places."

"What line are you in?"

He darted me a glance, instantly suspicious. "Finance," is what he eventually said.

"Ain't been easy," he said. "This was a chance for me to put a few things right. But I don't know." He scratched behind his ear. "Perhaps me and the kid have been away from each other too long."

"And his mother?"

He pulled a face and snorted like a pig. "Bitch," is what he said. "Thought she was a class act when I met her – spoke like she had a dick in her mouth. Turned out she was some whore from Bermondsey. You heard of that? Bermondsey?"

I nodded.

"Asshole of the empire. Kid's better off with me." He said this looking down into his beer trying to convince himself it was true.

I didn't say anything, just nodded sagely as if he spoke the universal truth about women and kids. "How long you got left?"

"Flight's booked in three days."

"Then home?"

His eyes strayed to his phone. "Ain't sure yet."

"Well if you still have a few days, maybe this is a chance to spend some quality time together. Paul likes fishing and I know a great place. The swimming and snorkelling is superb. And fish..." I opened my hands, measuring an imaginary catch. "Big. Paul would have a great time."

"Yeah?"

"Sure he would."

"I don't know."

"You'd enjoy it too. Be a chance for you and Paul to do something together."

He was hesitant, though I could see I had sown a seed of curiosity. All it needed was a gentle nudge to push him into my camp.

The nudge came from behind.

"Hey. You a Hoops man or what?"

The hoarse Glaswegian accent grated but I swivelled round on my stool to look. It was the big red-headed guy. He was holding court with his two buddies and had decided to expound his theories of what makes a man. And supporting a different team or being born on the wrong side of the border made you into a form of lesser being. For his benefit, I put on a puzzled look.

"Hoops?"

He frowned, though it could just as easily have been an attempt to focus.

"Aye. Hoops," and he leant forward and sneered as if the very word might send him to hell. "Celtic. Are you one a them?"

I feigned understanding and smiled. "No," I said, "I'm not."

The big man sniffed. He was moving on his seat, swaying back and forth as if he were on a train or bus. "What about you, Yank? What's yer team?"

"Hell's it gotta do with you?"

I wasn't sure whether the boys at the table heard but they heard something and squinted at Barry. I clamped a hand on his shoulder and gave Carrot Top my finest grin. "We're more fans of the oval ball."

"Eh?" He turned his baffled face back to me.

"Rugby," I said. "We follow Saracens."

He turned back to his companions and jeered. "Told ye. Rugby." For a moment I thought he was going to spit on the floor. "Pair of gay boys." The other two played along and grinned in their beers. Their eyes were shiny, heavy with the drink, and the sport was to their liking.

Barry shifted on his seat but a squeeze of his shoulder was enough to still him while I turned back to the bar and the mirror behind.

"Yeah, rugby," I said. "A proper man's game."

Through the glass I saw Carrot Top stiffen. "Nay – fitba's the game. Hey,

Mitch." He called to the barman. "Put the song on."

Mitch swivelled his eyes from me to the big man. Not sure how things were going to pan out, he ran a hand beneath the counter just to reassure himself that if things kicked off, countermeasures were in place. Satisfied, he went to the disc player and pressed play.

'Penny Arcade': the Rangers call to arms. Damn thing was probably on a loop.

As the opening bars ran through the speaker the big guy, closely followed by his mates, began to clap. Big, exaggerated movements, directed to where we were sitting. And at the chorus

– fists raised in the air and shouting – "Roll up and spend your last dime".

Barry glowered. The couple by the entrance, fellow Glaswegians I was sure, joined in. But if they were expecting an accompaniment from me they were very much mistaken. I smiled, moved my head back and forth like a jerk and looked on with an expression of mild amusement – just enough to piss him off. The song finished with a round of applause and Carrot Top rising from his seat to use the toilet at the end of the bar. As he passed, he knocked into my arm, spilling beer on to the counter.

"Ah, sorry, pal." And with that he turned to his mates, stuck his tongue between his teeth and winked.

I watched him wobble to the toilet and turned my head to Barry. He squirmed until his buttocks squeaked on the stool's vinyl.

"You hungry?" I asked.

"What?" Barry's forehead creased.

There was a menu on the counter. It was coated in Perspex, flat-edged and held inside a wooden stand so it stood straight as a soldier on parade.

Barry frowned. "Thought you said you had just eaten?"

I reached for it and shrugged. "Just looking."

From the toilet I heard the flush and the door bang open. Carrot Top was looking at me. He picked his near-empty glass off the table and came to stand at the bar on my left. He bent his head so that I caught the fetid air of his breath as well as his words. "English, are ye?"

I pulled my head back from his stink and began to tap the menu board on the counter. "English is right."

He swayed some more, drained the last of his beer, and when he poked me in the chest with a stubby, index finger I knew exactly where this was going.

"North sea oil," he said. "You took our Scottish oil and gave us the poll tax."

"Why don't you add Culloden as well and get it all in?"

"Fucking cunt." And with that he started to swing the empty glass. Holding it by his side, he brought it up in a wide arc and sought to crack it in my face. He was slow and telegraphed the move by baring his teeth. I blocked his arm using my left and still sitting on the stool jabbed the menu into his Adam's apple.

That stopped him. A strange gurgling, like water going down a drain, erupted from somewhere inside. A second later he dropped the glass and brought his hands to his throat. I was off the stool before the glass shattered on the floor.

The other two were moving. Worked out before Carrot Top went to the gents, they slid their legs from beneath the table and came at us; one at me the other for Barry. But Barry was no slouch. He too, was off his stool, fists up, and if that was the way of it, prepared to meet their violence head on.

He was also faced by the smallest of the three.

But I had no time to help for his "pal" came at me with a bottle. Well versed in the art of the pub brawl, these guys worked as a unit and were used to taking out others in much the same level of intoxication as themselves. But I hadn't drunk much, never did when I was on a job, and watched with grim amusement as he tried to crack me over the head. He led with his left, grabbed my shirt and made ready to make the blow. And in that moment he left himself exposed and vulnerable. His face was a wide area and a sharp jab with straight fingers into his eyes and a swerve to the left and his move went wild. The bottle smashed on the counter. Turning my head lest any slivers catch me, I saw Barry take two jabs to his face.

Okay, game over.

My opponent was still grasping my shirt, eyes red and streaming, too stupid or too lame in reactions to realise he couldn't see. I took hold of the hand on my shirt, twisted it to the left and down, almost breaking his wrist. At the same time I kneed him in the crotch. That did it. An expulsion of air escaped his lungs and he bent over, hands seeking balls pushed into his chest and throbbing like they were on fire.

That gave me the freedom to look to Barry.

Barry Evans was mean and nasty but no fighter. Bleeding from his nose, he took a wild swing at his opponent, missed and left himself off balance. The other saw and jabbed again. Barry turned and took a step back until the counter halted his retreat. Pinned against the bar there was no more going back. His opponent grimaced and moved in for the kill. I just had time. Carrot Top had stopped choking and was retching like a cat with a fur-ball.

I grabbed his arm and shirt and flung him at his mate. Arms

flailing, he careered into his pal, sending them both spinning away. Barry was panting. Looking across at me, he nodded his thanks and wiped a hand beneath his nose. Seeing the blood he paused, rubbed it between his fingers and slowly raised his eyes to the two guys who were trying to get themselves together. I watched Barry, watched his nostrils flair before a sly grin curled his lip. He slipped his hand into his back pocket and produced a knife. Holding it away from his body, he pressed the catch and the blade flicked out. He took one step forward.

Three great crashes, thuds so loud that I ducked, came from behind. Mitch had seen enough. Retrieved from beneath the counter, he brought the baseball bat down a fourth time then pointed it at Barry.

"No more!" he said. And there was no mistaking where the round end of that bat would go if Barry persisted.

There was a pause, a brief lull where the thing could have gone either way.

Slowly, hands held up to show I meant no harm, I moved to Barry's side. I laid a hand on the wrist that held the knife. I felt him stiffen, grip the knife harder, but I held on and whispered in his ear. "Not the time or place."

He darted me a glance. For a moment he looked confused, almost as if he didn't know where he was. Then he softened and I saw the light fall from his eyes.

"Yeah, yeah," he said and folded the blade back into the handle. He took a deep breath and pushed it back in his pocket.

I looked from Barry to the three pals and then to Mitch behind the bar. He was still gripping the baseball bat. Time to go. I tapped Barry and jutted my chin to the entrance. I moved slowly, keeping Barry between me and the boys, watching them as they watched us. Just as we passed the table with the young couple, Carrot Top stepped forward. Barry flinched but the only thing he held was his outstretched hand.

"Nay hard feelings, pal."

Barry looked at the hand then looked up and met the guy's eyes. "No," he said. "No hard feelings."

Slowly he began to raise his hand and meet that of Carrot Top. At the last moment he snatched an empty Magner's bottle by the neck and cracked it into the big man's face. Blood erupted from his nose. Mitch screamed and brought the baseball down on the counter again.

"Get out. Out!"

I grabbed Barry and shoved him away. Outside, we ran.

We stopped when Barry could run no more. Hands on his knees, head down, he was panting and wheezing. I looked back and patted him on the back. Raising is eyes, he followed my line of sight. Just for a moment there was a catch in his breath then, seeing there was no pursuit, he began to laugh. It was deep and rich and he shook his head as if he could hardly believe what had happened.

"That showed 'em,"he said.

"Sure did."

He stood straight and playfully punched me on the arm. "See that," he said and swung an imaginary bottle. "Caught him square, didn't I?"

"You did."

"I would have done the others too."

"Yeah."

He frowned. "You don't think I would have?"

I looked into his face – his bug eyes and self-satisfied grin. "Oh yeah," I said.

"I believe you would have taken them out. All the way out."

The creases on his forehead smoothed. He heard what he wanted to hear and pulling his shoulders back, stood a little straighter.

Content in the silence of our comradeship, neither of us spoke. Around us the bustle of the night continued. A bouquet of fried food, cheap perfume and the stink of humanity suffused the warm night with a unique aroma.

I reached in my pocket and produced a pack of handkerchiefs. "Here," I said.

"Clean your face before you go home to Paul." He took them, tore a wad from the opening and wiped his nose and chin. He dropped it on the floor then lit a cigarette.

"What you said before."

"About?"

"Going fishing with the boy. Were you serious?"

"Sure," I said. "If you want to."

"Could be good." He gestured with the cigarette. "A chance to re-acquaint ourselves."

"It's often the way, finding something you like to do together."

He nodded, almost thoughtful. "You got kids?"

I felt the air catch in my throat. It was a long time since I'd thought about

Michael. "No," I said. "No kids."

Barry dropped his stub and ground it into the pavement with his heel. He didn't say anything and I was glad. "Tomorrow then." And he held out his hand.

I took and squeezed it. "Tomorrow."

Barry grinned and turned to walk away. He took two steps then stopped.

"Hey," he shouted and held up a warning finger. "No pictures."

I held out my hands to show I had nothing but good intentions. "No. Nopictures," I lied.

*

We met by the harbour steps that led to the coastal path and Puerto Callero. I was there early and watched them come. Paul skipped, almost danced along the walkway while his father was slow, ponderous and in the cold light of morning, wondering what the hell he was doing. He was wearing the same khaki shorts and another Hawaiian shirt: same style, though this one was red. The guy must have bought a job lot from Wal-Mart. Paul had his rod and bag, Barry nothing. We shook hands and he stared at me, maybe still trying to fathom my motivation. There was a slight tinge of blue beneath his left eye and a cut on his lip, but all things considered, he didn't look too bad.

I looked down at Paul. "Ready to catch some fish?"

His eager face beamed, a big smile split his face, but his words caught as Barry landed a hand on his shoulder. "Sure thing. Paul can't wait." It was mark of his authority, a statement of ownership, and Barry was making sure I understood the rules. Picking up my bag and rods, I tipped my head upwards.

"Let's go then."

It was a steep climb. By the halfway mark Barry was blowing hard and had to stop. The guy was badly out of condition. Two flights ahead, Paul looked back with ill-disguised impatience. "C'mon, Dad. The day'll be over before you get there."

Barry looked at his boy then at me. He reached into the pocket of his shorts and pulled out a pack of cigarettes. "Maybe you two should go ahead. I'll catch you up."

I looked back at him and smiled. I knew enough about his character that once we were out of sight he would sneak back to the apartment and lay there for the rest of the day. That was not an option. "You'll be okay." I nodded to where Paul was leaning against the railing. "And I think Paul really wants you to come."

"Yeah?"

"Sure. He wants to show off – catch the biggest fish. Remember how he was when he caught yesterday?"

Barry nodded. "Yeah – yeah I do." He flicked the cigarette over the wall and took a deep breath. He shouted to Paul, "Don't think you're getting to the top before me." With that he set off at a run, loping up the steps two at a time until he caught up with Paul and began to race.

I followed at a steady pace, finding them both out of breath at the top. Ahead was a narrow boulevard shaded by pink and blue flowering shrubs that led to the cliff top. Below, the sea ran to a score of shades ranging from turquoise to the deepest blue. Barry was sweating. He formed a V with thumb and forefinger and drew it from brow to chin. Sweat ran from him like a tap. "How far?" he said.

I pointed, "Just up there. No more than ten minutes; I promise."

He followed my line of sight to where the boulevard turned to a dusty track.

The landscape was bleak: orange sand swirled in a breeze that raked the bare, volcanic rock.

"Well it'd better be or I'm doing one," and he jerked a thumb over his shoulder in an unmistakable sign of saying "I'm off".

"Dad." Paul looked at Barry and shook his head like he was dealing with a recalcitrant child. And looking from one to the other, I wondered just who the child was.

It was exactly ten minutes.

On the point where the path dipped out of sight, a derelict, fisherman's cottage stood on the cliff. Roofless and with only three walls standing, it had been built too close to the edge. Subsidence or earth tremors in the distant past had made habitation too perilous and it had been left to ruin and decay. In a corner a few empty beer bottles and dog-ended spliffs showed that this was the in place to hang out. And from what I'd seen of the bars downtown, it oozed as much class.

Beyond the empty window frame, a path led to the cliff edge where steps had been cut into the rock. At the bottom was a horseshoe bay.

Barry stood on the top and looked. "Down there?"

"Only way," I said and he glanced across to see if I was serious. Paul was already out of sight.

"Hey," he called after him. "Be careful."

I looked over the edge. Excited, he was almost running down the steps. Just for a moment I felt something inside. It was a strange sensation – fear perhaps, maybe it was concern for something other than myself. Either that or it was the paella from the night before.

But I shouted anyway. "Slow down, Paul. Those steps can be slippy." He nodded but continued in the same vein, his only concession a hand held against the rock wall to steady himself. I smiled. The kid knew no fear.

We took it a little steadier. I offered to follow Barry but he insisted on coming behind. I could hear him clumping, one step at a time, and cursing beneath his breath until we got to the bottom where a rocky cove sloped gently to the sea. Paul was already halfway to getting set up. Rod angled against one of the many boulders that lay around the bay, he was threading the line through its rings.

I dropped my bag in the shade of the overhanging cliff and decided to use my spinning rod. It took seconds. I selected a silver lure fitted with treble hooks and tied it to the line. A moment later I was fishing, casting out and drawing it back, probing the water with each successive cast in a bid to entice that elusive fish. The water was deep here – very deep. From the water's edge, a shelf plunged down thirty, maybe forty feet to the bottom. Barry stayed in the shade and ran his tongue over his dry lips.

He looked at my bag. "You got a drink in there?"

I slapped a hand against my forehead. "Damn. I knew I'd

forgotten something." We both looked at Paul. He had just finished tying his hook. "Did you bring any water?"

Better organised, he rooted in his bag until he came up with a half-litre bottle.

He threw it to his dad. Barry looked at it, sipped, then drank until half of it was gone.

"Paul," I said and reached in my pocket. "There's a Mercado by the harbour."

I waved a twenty euro note. "Will you run back and get some water?"

His face fell. It felt like I had stuck a pin in his side. All the excitement that had built up leaked away like air through a faulty valve. He looked at the water then at his dad. Barry reached into his trouser pocket and pulled out some euros. "I've got it."

"No, it's my fault," I said and pushed the note into Paul's hand. He looked at the water. "Don't worry, the sea will still be here when you get back." He looked at the money. "Get some coke and crisps for yourself. The way you run, it'll take you fifteen minutes tops." I winked. "And I promise not to catch any fish till you get back."

He looked to Barry, seeking his permission. He nodded and clapped his hands.

"Be quick. I'm dyin' of thirst here."

Paul took off, shot up the steps two at a time and ran like the wind. Once he got to the top he was lost from view.

So now it was just Barry and me – and the sea and the rocks and the wind.

We looked at each other.

Barry's eyes never left my face. He was thinking, wondering, and just as I was about to cast my line, he made up his mind and reached into his side pocket. The flap was held down by a stud and it seemed to be stuck for he grimaced and twisted until it came free. He pulled out a gun, a small revolver. Where the hell he got it from is anyone's guess and whether it was real or a replica I didn't know. But he pointed it at me as if he knew what he was doing.

"Okay," he said. "Now you're going to be straight with me. Is it me or the boy you're interested in?"

"You."

"Figures. Haven't trusted you from the start – too friendly.

But I didn't take you for a pervert. So what is it you're after: information – money?" He cocked his head to one side. "Or is this more serious?"

That's when I flicked the rod and sent the lure spinning towards his face. He ducked, dodged the spinner but didn't realise I was aiming at the hand holding the gun. One of the hooks snagged his wrist. He yelped as I yanked and the gun dropped from his hand. I pulled again reeling him in like a prize specimen until the hook ripped through his skin and he fell to his knees.

"Goddamn it." He stood there holding a hand over the cut while blood dripped from his wrist.

Watching him to make sure he didn't run, I reached into the bag and removed the semi-automatic. It was a Beretta 92, silencer already snapped in place. I pointed it at him. "As I said, it's you I'm interested in."

"I knew it; I knew you weren't on the level. God." He beat his hand against his head. "Stupid – stupid!" He looked at me, looked at the gun and began to chew his lip. "So this – is really serious?"

I nodded.

"Who was it: Mulligan – Kepler?"

"Madera."

"Madera!" The inflection that raised his voice an octave told me Madera wasn't even on his radar – a figure forgotten even in his degenerate mind. He shook his head and looked away. "Jesus – Madera." His brows knitted and he looked at me. "You know why?"

"Don't you?"

He laughed; shallow and forced it was an expression of defeat. "Yeah," he said. "I know why." He spat on the floor. "Anything I can do?"

"No."

"Didn't think so." He took a deep breath and looked away. "How's it to be?"

"In the face." I shrugged. "Madera was quite specific."

He was silent for a few seconds while the words sank in. "Don't like that," he said and looked back at me – looked me right in the eye and didn't flinch. "Couldn't you do me from behind first. After," and he shrugged, "you could put one in from the front. Wouldn't matter then."

I didn't answer, it seemed unnecessary. I just held the gun steady and met his eye with what I guessed was a cold-blooded stare.

"Yeah, well," he said at last and looked away, fingers rubbing against each other as if the answer to his dilemma were somehow within reach. A thought came and his fingers stopped moving. "What about the boy?"

"I'll look after things."

His lips twitched. "I bet you will." He shook his head. "I didn't like the kid much anyway."

And that did surprise me. "What?"

"I said I never did like him." He waved a hand around the side of his head.

"Too fanciful, head full of garbage just like his mother. I'm not even sure he is mine." He shook his head. "She never could keep her mouth or legs shut, know what I mean?"

My finger tightened on the trigger.

And then his mouth dropped and he clapped a hand to his head. "It was her, wasn't it? Was it she who put you on to me – declaring open season just so she could get the kid back?" He looked at me, his face full of fury and anger. "She owes me big time, did you know that? I wasn't going to hurt the kid." He shrugged. "Just some leverage to get what's mine."

I held his gaze for a few seconds. To Barry Evans it must have seemed a lifetime. I dropped the hammer and let the gun drift to my side. "Yeah," I said. "You're right. She put me onto you. And it's not Madera. It's Ellen."

Evans froze. I saw the sudden raising of spirit, the hope where there was no hope before.

"Ellen?"

"She says if you send the boy back and get out of her life there'll be no repercussions."

"Take him back?"

I shrugged. "Or I'll take him back." I held the gun up. "This was to show she means business."

His head slumped forward and a long breath, held in for so long, whistled through his teeth. "Ellen – Christ." He shook his head wondering how his life had got so fucked up that his wife – ex-wife – wanted him dead. "Just send him back?"

"That's it."

"I can do that," he said quietly. And now when he looked at me there was a glimmer in his eye I'd not noticed before. "Yeah, I can do that." The moment had passed, ideas and dreams that so recently lay like trash in the gutter of his life began to emerge with a startling new clarity. He thought for a moment then glanced across at me, his eyes slyly gauging my reaction. "Unless..."

"Unless?"

He shrugged. "Maybe I don't have to. I've been waiting on a phone call." He reached into his pocket and I pulled the gun up to cover him. Using thumb and forefinger he produced his mobile. "I ain't gonna get it, am I?"

I shook my head.

"But maybe," and he shrugged and lowered his voice as if the world were listening. "Maybe you and I could come to an arrangement?"

"Arrangement?"

"Tell me what she's paying and I'll better it – double it," he said quickly.

"You tell her I can't be found. She puts the money into my account and I'll send the boy back on the next flight."

Even now the guy wanted to do a deal. Slowly I shook my head. "I'm doing her a favour."

His eyes narrowed. "People in your line don't do favours." Then his face cleared and the slyness returned. "You're screwing her, aren't you?" He laughed, a single roar as if he couldn't believe it. "Man," he said. "I hope you know what you're doing. She'll screw you in more ways than one." He spat on the floor then looked at me. "What if I don't."

"You'll do the right thing."

He smiled. "Yeah, sure I will." Ideas were already forming. He got up off his knees, began to wipe himself down, and that's when I shot him. In the face like Madera had told me to.

Back in the day Ellen and I were friends – lovers even. When I discovered her connection to Evans I went to see her. Bastard had snatched Paul a week before and was demanding money. She agreed to help. Just so long as I got the boy back. Obviously she didn't know my reputation for tying up loose ends.

I watched Barry Evans, Johnny Gee or whatever his name

was, collapse. I was using a 9mm and from this range it blew out the back of his head. He went down like a sack of shit thrown from a lorry.

Quickly I scanned the rocks and the cliff above. Hidden by the overhang, it would have been unlucky if anyone saw. Still, I worked quickly. Using my phone I took three pictures: two from the front and one side view – I'd send them to Madera then destroy the phone. From behind one of the giant boulders that lined the cove, I took the length of rope and weight secreted earlier that morning, tied a hitch knot around his leg, attached the other end to the weight and rolled him over the ledge into five fathoms of water. In a day or two he would give some nosy diver the fright of their life and a story to keep them in beer for a long, long time. Either that or the fish would dine well until the rope frayed and his decomposed body washed up on some distant beach. But I would be gone by then. I had a ticket from Arrecife tomorrow morning and any search for Adam Sadler would come to a dead end.

There was a little blood on the rocks and I had just finished sluicing it down when I heard Paul's breathless voice calling from the steps behind. Clutching a plastic bag in one hand, he was racing down. He came over and scanned the area before his puzzled face settled on mine.

"I'm sorry, Paul, but your dad's had to go."

"Go?"

"He got that call he was waiting for." I shrugged. "He just couldn't wait."

Paul's face fell and he looked at the rocks beneath his feet. It was a lame story and I wouldn't have expected him to believe it excepting his father or the man he thought was his father had done it so many times before. I frowned and looked at Paul's face – that familiarity was bugging me. I started to do some mental arithmetic.

"But," said Paul and pointed back up the steps. "I would have seen him. He would have passed me."

"He went into Puerto Callero and got a taxi from there. It's closer. Anyway, he asked me to keep an eye on you." I took out my phone. "And asked me to call your mum." At mention of his mother, Paul's face lit up. I scrolled down my directory and speed-dialled Ellen's number. She answered immediately. I played the part then handed the phone to Paul while I walked away. I heard him giggle, heard his excited explanation of where he had been and what he had done and heard him say "I love you". Not bad for a twelve year old. He was missing her. I swallowed the lump in my throat. Jeez, what was happening to me? Still holding the phone to his ear, Paul came over.

"Mum wants to speak to you."

I took the phone, nodded, and gave one-word answers to her questions and told her I'd be on the plane with Paul tomorrow. Just before she rang off, she thanked me again. "What you've done," she said, "well I don't know how I'll ever be able to thank you."

I told her it was okay, but I already had a few things on my mind – the truth for one thing. She ended the call.

I looked at my watch. "Well," I said to Paul. "We've got an early flight tomorrow but if you want, I reckon we can still get a couple of hours' fishing in."

He liked that and ran to fetch his rod.

As he came back I pointed along the cove. "Let's try over there," I said. "The fishing's not so good here. And as I clapped him on the shoulder and steered him away from the water's edge, I looked down and smiled. Maybe this was one loose end that could wait a while – at least until I saw his mother.

Fake

Capo was giving it large, boasting of how he'd robbed the off-licence and flaunting his new-found wealth in front of those he nominally called friends. He cracked another tin of lager, waved it in Ricky's face until it frothed from the opening and he had to slurp quickly lest any be lost.

"'Seasy," he said. "Walked in, pulled out the shooter," he made his free hand into the shape of a gun, "and said, 'Give us the money, darling, or this thing's liable to go off.'"

He took another swig from the can and wiped his nose free of the white residue that clung to his nostrils like anaemic snot.

"Yeah, easy street."

He put his hand into his back pocket, held up a wad of cash.

Capo had scored big then purchased three cases of lager and 5g of coke from a dealer he knew in the Inglenook. He threw what was left from Bargain Booze's till across the coffee table.

"You really said that?"

Tricia's eyes were wide in admiration as she sipped from a can delicately poised in her fat fingers. She was sprawled on a leather sofa that had more patches on its arms than an ex-smoker craving nicotine in what Capo laughingly called his "pad". The flat was as squalid as himself – the bed hadn't been changed in months and the sink was piled with dirty dishes. But to Capo, it was home.

He looked at Tricia's tits bulging beneath her white tank top and grabbed his crotch.

"Yeah. Just like this thing's liable to go off."

She put a hand to her mouth, laughed like a hyena giving birth.

Sitting opposite, Ricky stifled a yawn. He had drunk six cans and the effectsfrom the two lines of coke were wearing off. He wanted to sleep. Last night his old man had been going on and on at him – "no job, no money, a lazy fucking layabout" – so much that he had stormed out and roamed the streets till the early hours. All he wanted to do was close his eyes. But he needed to stay sharp, for he knew all about Capo's little tricks.

He smiled falsely, looked across the room; Trish on the sofa, Capo on its arm, worming his way in, and both laughing like they shared some joke he wasn't privy to. He and Trish had an understanding. That's what he thought, and while it would never be a meeting of minds, he'd settle for a corruption of bodies that went far beyond his limited experience of women and owed more to an expansive imagination than was a given fact. He was just waiting for the right time. The right time to make his move.

He watched Tricia toss back hair that fell in a rivulet of black tresses and flutter long, false lashes in a semaphore display of availability. And from where he sat, he could see up her skirt. It barely covered her arse anyway, but every so often he got a tantalising flash of white knickers. Ricky swallowed. It sent his brain into overdrive.

He lifted his can, finished what was left, crushed it in his fist. "A gun," he said and nodded sagely. "That's the way to go. 'Course, when I was in the game, we had to use whatever came to hand." And he smiled a sabre-toothed grin he thought would impress the girl. "Sometimes naked steel is enough to make 'em wet their pants."

Ricky had done nothing more than nick beer from the offie and piss in public. But with Trish enraptured by Capo's daring deeds, felt he had to say something to promote his worth.

"Is right, lad, is right." Capo rose from his perch and made a fist. "Give 'em fear and you can do anything." Pulling a plastic baggy from his pocket, he split the knot with his teeth and poured the white powder on the glass table next to Ricky. Cutting it into three thin lines with the craft blade set there for just such a purpose, he rolled a £20 note into a thin tube and snorted the first line. He was showing off and loving it. "Go 'head," he said, and handed Ricky the twenty. "Have one on me."

Ricky leaned forward. He had already taken more than enough but was damned if he was going to refuse. Not with Tricia looking. Bending over the table, he snorted through his right nostril. The powder hit the back of his throat. He grunted, sniffed three or four times, flicked his nose with his fingers before closing his eyes and settling back in his chair. Even more than the first and second, this hit the mark. It was like standing on a beach and having the salt sea spray wash over him. His momentary lethargy evaporated as wave after wave of energy swept through him. Ricky's vision cleared to a point where anything was possible.

He opened his eyes. Capo had left the room. Still sitting on the couch, Tricia had folded her legs beneath her. Ricky followed the contours of her body and focused on her pasty thighs. Like a pair of albino pythons, they slithered up her skirt. He felt a throb in his groin. It spread through him, his mind playing with the sweet fantasies he had conjured on many a lonely night in his room. He should take her now, put his hands on those supple, soft titties; fuck her like she'd never been fucked before.

Tricia saw him looking.

"What?"

Ricky grinned, felt the narcotic buzz surging through his veins. This was it, the moment had arrived. And he knew with absolute conviction that all he had to do was say the word. All he had to do was...

The gun landed on the table beside him. He jerked back, eyes filled with an image of chrome and steel. "Fuck's sake Capo." He came down quickly. "Thing could have gone off."

"Don't think so. It's not real see." He looked at Tricia, winked. "Unlike me, it only fires blanks."

Ricky leaned forward, scrutinised the revolver. "Looks real enough."

"That's the point. Wave that in someone's face and they're liable to give you what you want."

"Yeah?"

"Wouldn't you?"

Ricky pursed his lips. He could see Capo's point.

"Borrow it if you like."

Ricky looked from the gun to Capo, wondering if he was winding him up.

Tricia barked a laugh. "Him? He hasn't got the bottle." She went over, ruffled his hair. "Have you love?" She kissed his ear then went to Capo and put her arm around his waist. "Not like you, is he?"

Ricky felt the heat in his face, burning with the indignity of having Tricia ridicule him in front of Capo. Reaching forward he picked up the pistol. It was different from what he expected, almost like an extension of his arm.

Capo whistled. "Look at him. He's a natural."

Tricia snorted.

Ricky looked at the sleek, silver weapon in his hand. "I

could, y'know." He closed one eye, levelled the gun, swept it around the room. Here was power, a power he had never felt before, and he saw himself in the foyer of the bank where they had knocked back his loan application. The thought of pushing the gun into the backs of those smug suited vipers, while Tricia – Bonnie to his Clyde – rushed from till to till filling bags with cash, filled with a kind of ecstasy. A fast getaway, a night on the town then a hotel suite where she'd open her arms and legs, and tell him he was a hero.

Sweet. He gazed into the distance, lost in a dream of what could be. He jumped as Capo slapped his shoulder.

"Course you could," he said. "You've got the balls." He stood back and gestured to the gun. "The means, and with your experience it'd be like..."

"Taking candy from a baby." Tricia beamed.

"Yeah." Capo said and winked at her. "That's it. Just like that."

Ricky looked up to see his friends grinning like he'd won the lottery. "You mean I should do it?"

"Absolutely."

"Where?"

"Bookie's on Park Street. Thought about it meself but," Capo shrugged, "if you want a piece of it." He made that same open-handed gesture Ricky had seen so many times and that was as genuine as Katie Price's tits.

"What's in it for you?"

"Hey, we're pals." The hurt in Capo's voice didn't wash, so Ricky waited until Capo grinned. "But I'm supplying the gun. So for a small fee..."

Ricky nodded, made sense. Capo did nothing without some ulterior motive. He turned the gun in his hand. Its weight was a comfort, its threat awesome. He looked up, saw Capo and Tricia exchange glances. There was something...

He shook his head. No. As Capo said, they were pals. "Just go in there and do it?"

"You wave that bit of kit, there's no one going to stand in your way."

Tricia came over and stroked the nape of his neck. "And with the score you're gonna make, we could have a good time." She whispered in a way that could have only one meaning. "A real good time."

Ricky's heart skipped then beat to a new rhythm – that of opportunity. "So this Bookie's," he said, "when's the best time to hit it?"

*

According to Capo, the best time was now, while the idea was hot and the body willing. And while Ricky prevaricated, rubbed his chin, and said he should think about it some more, Trish and Capo had pushed the point to such an extent that here he was, outside Ladbroke's, with a gram of coke inside him and a shooter in the back of his kecks. But what else could he have done? For once, Tricia had looked at him like he was the man.

So Ricky took a deep breath, pulled up the hood of his jacket, and walked right in. He stopped by the door, scanned the room. Felt like everyone had their eyes on him: the guy making his selections, the two studying the Racing Post, and the old boy sat in front of the TV. And then there was the girl in the booth – the girl with a Baywatch body and a Crimewatch face. She most of all.

Looked like she was expecting to be robbed.

Ricky swallowed. He knew what he should do. He should walk to the booth, stick the gun in her face and...

"'Scuse pal."

His heart thumped. Some guy had come in, placed a hand on his shoulder, and eased himself past. Ricky stepped aside, mumbled something incoherent beneath his breath. The big guy went straight to the booth and pushed his betting slip through the window.

Ricky shook himself. That was the way. He took a pen off the shelf, pretended to study the runners and riders then went to scribble on a betting slip. Fingers twitched. He clenched his fist, tried again. Better. He wrote big then put the pen down. The voice in his head said do it. He stared at the booth, brushed the gun in the back of his pants. But what was once natural and comforting now felt alien and hostile. And all the while his brain screamed at him to be a man. Ricky breathed deep. Do it, do it – the words in his head matched the rhythm of his steps. Closer now, so close that the glass-fronted booth filled his entire vision and the girl was Charon at the river, and he knew that once he had made that crossing, he could never, ever go back. He paused while she regarded him with eyes dull as dishwater, waiting for him to push the betting slip through the booth's window.

Hand moving independently of thought, Ricky laid it before her. The girl glanced at the note, frowned, and read it again. And as he stood there feeling naked and alone, he watched her lips moving in sync with the words. He guessed she was trying to interpret what "GIVE ME THE MONEY" actually meant.

Ricky waited till she looked up and brought her eyes level with his. This was the moment to make his play. Reaching back, he pulled the gun. The barrel caught, and as he fumbled it clear, it dropped to the floor. "Shit."

The girl groaned. This wasn't the first time. In fact Ladbroke's had been held up so many times, locals referred to it as the Cash & Carry. She closed her eyes, slapped her head. Why did it always happen to her?

Ricky retrieved the pistol from the floor and pointed it through the gap in the window. Surprised when the girl didn't shit herself or fall over backwards, he gestured her to hurry.

She placed an elbow on the counter, cupped her chin, and looked at him as if he were some kind of pond life. "What?" She thrust the word at him like a dagger.

Ricky cleared his throat, tried to sound mean. But when he opened his mouth, it came out high-pitched and whiney. Like a girl. "The money," he said. "Give it me now."

The girl let out a low sigh, opened the till, and went first to the twenties then the tens, and finally the fives. She gathered them together, placed them in three separate piles on the counter. Ricky's eyes widened. So much. He grinned, almost forgot where he was. Wanted to gaze on that filthy money forever.

Ricky snapped out of it. The gun had drifted until it and his hand rested on the counter. He waved it at the girl, gestured her to push the cash through the window. There were so many £10 notes she had to use both hands, squash them flat. Ricky went to grab it, stopped.

It wouldn't fit in his pockets. Not all of it. And he was left with the thought of running away with a stream of the Queen's currency following him like a public school paper trail. A bag. He needed a bag. Why hadn't he brought a bag?

Shit, shit and shit.

His tongue felt like sandpaper in a mouth worn dry by his stupidity. Just for a moment, he dared turn his head. Now all eyes were watching him. Laughing at him. Watching him with a quiet ambivalence that defied the fact he was holding a gun. He wanted to shout, pull the trigger, shake them out of their stupor and watch them cower beneath tables and chairs. Ricky's eyes darted from one to another, his anger growing with the sight of each dumb face. He clenched his teeth, swung the gun in a wide arc. Why weren't they scared? Did they know it was fake, a clone masquerading as the real thing? Did they know he was? His heart hammered. From the TV, the commentator's voice rose to a climax. Red Bobbin jumped the last fence a nose in front of Stargazer, and as they entered the final furlong so did Ricky. He saw salvation in a plastic bag lying on the floor. The winning post beckoned.

"Give me that." He pointed the gun at the old guy.

"What?"

Ricky jabbed the gun. "That."

The old man looked at him with the eyes of a man who's seen it all before. He frowned and peered beneath his chair. "This?" He lifted the Tesco bag off the floor.

"Yeah."

"Got a hole in it you know."

"I don't give a flying fuck if it's got a hole." Ricky's voice rose. He was almost screaming. "Just give it us."

The guy held it out.

Snatching it from his hand, Ricky turned back to the booth. The money sat there like birds ready to take flight. He swept the money into the bag, watched as a bundle fell through the hole. Ricky cursed. Why did everything he did always end in a fuck-up? He put the gun between his knees, tied a knot in the bag, went down on all fours picking up every wayward note, every last fiver. Not one was going to escape, not one was going to get away. Not now, not after he had worked this hard.

Mumbling to himself, he pushed the last inside before remembering where he was.

Ricky jerked upright, waved the gun in case anyone was thinking of being a hero. They weren't. In fact they were impatient for him to go so that they could get back to the more important events of the afternoon: the racing at Exeter and Kempton. Ricky curled his lip into his finest snarl, backed away to the door. Reaching behind, he pulled it open and slipped outside. A cold wind chilled the sweat on his face.

He had done it.

Ricky closed his eyes. Jesus Christ, he'd really done it. The rush was better than anything, ever, and that included the skag Capo sold him last week. But there was no time to bask in glory, he had to move. Looping the plastic bag around his wrist and pushing the gun in his waistband, Ricky started to walk. Past the burger bar and newsagent, past the off-licence and chippy, and all the time he was waiting for some loud voice to start screaming, somebody to point and yell thief. Nothing happened. He glanced back. All quiet. Cars rolled towards town. Women gossipped. People came and went from the supermarket. It was like a Sunday when he went to fetch the papers for his dad. .

He quickened his pace, headed for the parking spec Capo said he would be in. A cold chill ran through him. The car wasn't there – he wasn't there. Ricky slowed, looked again. There was a car but it was a different colour and make. And no one sat behind the wheel. Fear began to spread like oil on water. He had a bag full of cash and a gun in his pants. And even if it was fake, would the bizzies know? He sneered at himself. What if they did? A no-mark like him, it'd be shoot first, ask questions later.

Thoughts raced through his head. He could dump the gun and leg it. Tell Capo he lost it in a struggle or that he got jumped. Then again he could just fuck off and not go back. He bit his lip, weighed his options before a police patrol exiting the street next to Kwik-Save made everything simple. Ricky's breath caught in his throat. The squad car paused at the junction. Too soon. The Jacks couldn't know, not yet surely? And then a thought forced its way into his head. Maybe that was it. Maybe Capo had seen the patrol and took off. The squad car indicated and turned away. He had to move, and quickly.

Passing between two parked cars he crossed the road and headed in the opposite direction, towards the pebble-dashed walls of the housing estate. Every instinct told him to run, but even as he heard the siren, even as his heart skipped and his breath came in ragged gasps, he forced himself to walk. 'Don't look, don't look,' he said, repeating the words over and over until his self-serving mantra was lost in the siren's call, and he at last risked a glance behind. Ricky's legs almost gave way. The patrol car hadn't stopped. It hadn't gone to Ladbroke's or stopped to ask the witnesses a thousand stupid questions. It had swerved the scene of the crime, left the details for some other blue-nosed cunt to define, and was bearing down on him like a banshee from hell. Self-preservation kicked in. Ricky ran.

Before it followed him around the corner, he ducked behind a parked car. As it passed he clocked the occupants. The driver, older, more experienced, swivelled his head left and right, watching for any movement that might give him away. In the passenger seat, a young Turk. Keen, ready for action, his shaved, bullet-shaped head jutted forward, eyes bulging from the thrill of the chase.

Ricky let it pass then ran to the estate where an open door or a friendly face might offer a lifeline. But doors had closed and any friendly face had turned away to watch the action from an upstairs window. Ricky's heart beat wildly. He had dodged one patrol but there would be others. Matrix, the armed response unit, would be on their way and soon the estate would be crawling with police. He had to get off the street. In front of him was a six-foot wooden fence leading to the back gardens. Ricky tied a knot in the bag, threw it over and heaved himself after it. He landed heavily, felt something in his ankle give and went down in a heap. More sirens echoed in the distance. Sitting up, he winced, felt his ankle. Sore, but manageable. For a moment the police would be blind but that wouldn't last. He had to go before they threw a blanket over the area and cut off every avenue of escape. If he could make his way through the estate and then across the park, he could lose himself in the back streets. And Capo would be there. Didn't he say if it went tits up to go to the second rendezvous point? Ricky frowned. Seemed so long ago now.

Whatever, he had no time to think. Gathering himself he lunged for the first fence, pulled himself over. Using the gardens like stepping-stones, Ricky jumped each wooden fence in succession. As he did, he scanned each and every window for the face that might give him away. He was lucky, only once was he seen. But the old girl, who had a mouthful of pegs and her hands full of linen, just stared at him like he was some kind of apparition. By the time she thought and considered her options he was gone.

Ricky paused. He had made it to the last house on the estate. One of the big ones, three bedrooms and gardens front and rear. In front of him was the access road that curled round and joined the through route. If he could cross it, gain access to the private houses lining the main road, he had a chance.

Ricky started. Three kids, aged six or seven at most, watched from the front garden. Any second now he just knew one was just going to start bawling. Ricky put on a big smile and held a finger to his lips. Two of the kids ran. Crouched down behind a rose bush, slick with sweat, he probably looked like Jack the Ripper. And he felt like shit. Ricky pulled down his hood, wiped his face. One kid still stood there, watching. He forced another smile. "Hey mate," he said. "Are the bizzies out there?"

The boy looked at him. He was blond and blue-eyed with a mass of curls. A beautiful kid, an angelic kid; and he held out a hand for his cut of the take.

"Jesus." Ricky shook his head. Even the kids were on the fucking make. He untied the bag, handed the kid a £10 note.

The boy turned it in his hand but didn't move. Ricky felt like giving him a slap. Instead he slipped his hand back in the bag and produced another £10 note. The boy smiled, went to take it, but Ricky was too quick and snatched it away. He waved it in the kid's face.

"Do I look soft? You get this when you come back."

The boy narrowed his eyes, wondered if Ricky was legit. Finally satisfied, he ran out of view. A few seconds later he came back, shook his head. Ricky's heart leapt. A chance. Cash bag stuffed under his jacket, gun weighing him down like an anchor, he crawled from the undergrowth and went to slip away. The kid tugged his jacket. Ricky looked at him.

"This what you want?" He showed the £10 note to the kid then bent low so he was right in the boy's face. "Well tough fucking luck." He pushed past, walked the garden path as if he had been visiting friends.

Checking left and right he crossed the road. A patrol car flashed past at the end of the street just as the kid began to wail. Running into the front drive of the house opposite he ducked down behind the bins. One more garden, one more road then the park and freedom. And even if Capo wasn't there he could lose himself in a tangle of back streets the police could never hope to lock down. A screech of tyres checked his dreams. Spinning blue lights filled his vision. A patrol car slid to a halt in the gutter. Inside was the older cop and young Turk. Ricky had just time to see the side door open and his bullet-shaped head appear before he ran and leapt the wooden fence.

Dropping down, Ricky heard him stumble on the gravel. But he had no time to gloat. In his haste to clear the fence, he landed on his bad ankle. Pain shot through him. No time. He yelped, hobbled through the gate, dodged the cars, and ran for the park. Behind, banging his fist on the fence in frustration and shouting at him to "Stop" and that he was a "cunt", was the red-faced cop. Like that was going to work. Ricky turned his head in time to see him drop out of sight. There would be a minute, vital seconds, while he joined his buddy in the car and made the turn out of the estate.

Ricky kept to the edge of the park. He was hurting but, if he could make it across this open space, was almost home. And every second, he was putting distance between himself and the chase. Ricky walked the last few metres. Three stone steps by the Belvedere Arms led to Blackburn Street. He calmed himself. The sound of pursuit faded. Sirens still wailed in the distance and no doubt the pack of patrol cars were circling the estate like wolves scenting blood. But here was an oasis of calm. It wouldn't last. The cop with the shaven head had seen where he was headed and soon a flood of vehicles would follow.

But now Ricky had options. This was home, a warren of interlocking streets where a rat could go to ground and never be found. He set off, felt his leg begin to stiffen as he turned into Griton Street but didn't care. Capo's car sat at the kerb only a hundred metres away.

He had done it: held up the bookie's, made off with the cash, and gotten away with it. This was the best day of his life. Tricia was right – he was the man.

Ricky had taken no more than two steps when he froze. Something inside him, the feral sense of the thief perhaps, made him stop and listen. He cocked his head. In the distance he could hear a car, its engine gunning as it raced through the gears. And then it came.

The squad car screeched round the corner, the driver

hitting the brakes hard – so hard it dipped, fishtailed side to side and squealed on the tarmac. It slid to a stop blocking the road behind him. He turned to run, saw a cop dart from the side street in front of him. It was the bullet-headed Turk, the twat who had dogged him from the very start. He was panting, breathing heavy, but there was a gleam in his eye and a grin on his face.

Trapped.

Ricky groaned, clutched his head and squeezed. No way, no way was he going to fall at the last. He gritted his teeth. As the Jack went for his taser, Ricky reached for the pistol, held it like he knew what he was doing. Yet still the cop came, still he had but one thing on his mind: make the arrest and be the toast of the nick.

Ricky levelled the pistol, cocked the hammer like he'd seen in so many films and pointed it at the bizzie's head. Surely that would make him think? Behind the cop's shoulder, he saw Capo. He was out of the car, eyes wide in his thin face, waving and shouting.

But Ricky had gone too far to back down.

All he wanted was to frighten him, all he wanted was enough room to slip by and escape. The sound of a blank was no different from the real thing. That's what Capo had said. And even if it wasn't, it would be enough to put the shits up the cunt. Ricky had never fired a gun, never before wanted to. He closed his eyes even as he pulled the trigger.

The noise was astounding. His eyes sprang open as the shock wave reverberated through his head and rang in his ears. When he looked, the bizzie's face was surrounded by a fine red mist. As it cleared, Ricky saw the hole. The hollow-point .22 had created a circle of raw meat where his mouth and nose had been. The cop stood for a few seconds then sank to his knees. Finally, he fell face forward on the hard surface of the road.

Ricky looked at the gun in his hand, at the smoking barrel, at the chamber that contained real bullets. Behind him the cop was out of the car, eyes blank and staring at a something he couldn't believe. Capo had turned away and was climbing into the car. Ricky stared. Through the rear windscreen, he could see Tricia. For a moment she held his gaze, then her long black lashes flashed, and she turned her head.

At last the ringing in Ricky's ears cleared. Beneath a sky

of gunmetal grey, the shot's echo still lingered. The cop lay in the road and didn't move. Capo's car roared into life and Ricky's world collapsed. He needed him, needed him more than ever. But Capo didn't look back. He burnt rubber and screeched from the kerb.

Ricky looked again at the gun. Acid burned his throat, and as he turned aside to vomit, he tossed it in the gutter. And as he retched, the truth pulsed from his guts in nauseating spasms of green bile. And knowing didn't make it any easier. There was only one fake on the street today.

And the truth wasn't any comfort. No comfort at all.

Part of the Deal

He was cold and naked and tied to a chair. Cable ties cut into his wrists and blood seeped from his nose. But that wasn't the worst. Michael Taylor's guts spasmed and he dry-heaved again. There was nothing left, his stomach was empty and the semi-digested contents of his last meal lay at his feet. Michael spat on the floor. He had expected pain but this – this brought suffering to the level of art. Slowly he raised his head. Swinging from a piece of flex, a single bulb illuminated the cellar. Somewhere behind were the men who had inflicted such torture. In other circumstances, he might have admired them.

Michael tried to swallow but his throat was raw and, as he gagged again, his head slumped. He had talked – of course he had talked – and now he was left shamed and embarrassed with the one thought that never again would he make love to his wife. He was going to die – was prepared to feel the cold touch of steel on the back of his neck and the quick trip to oblivion that awaited him. He just hoped he could look his killer in the eye and not piss himself.

Michael Taylor closed his eyes. It had taken one day, just one day for the whole of his world to unravel.

And it could have been so different.

*

The plastic seat in the airport lounge was hard, uncomfortable and obviously designed for a midget. Michael shifted his weight and felt his backside slide on the shiny surface. Once more he glanced at the Arrivals board. The flight from Schiphol was late. He settled back, squirmed to get comfortable and took a roll of X-tra Strong mints from his jacket pocket. He closed one eye. How long was it since he'd last enjoyed a cigarette? Three – four weeks? Michael looked at the peppermint in his hand with an air of disdain. It was at least four weeks – had to be. But it was good, good that he'd stopped, and he popped the sweet in his mouth and waited for the flavour to hit. But it wasn't the same; he still missed his smokes. In truth he would never have bothered but for Jan and the baby. Jan was Jan but Emily was only four and already on his case. He shook his head but an easy smile came too. Michael always said he wasn't the marrying kind – guessed he still wasn't. But when Jan told him she was pregnant he had done the right thing. And when Emily was born he realised she was the best thing that had ever happened to him. He thought of her now: her blonde curls and cheeky laugh. She was his, a real daddy's girl, and Michael would do anything for her.

He checked his watch again. He shouldn't be nervous. Connor had told him not to be nervous. The guy he was meeting represented concerns in the US and knew nothing about the recent unpleasantness. Michael bit down on the mint and felt it fracture. This time Connor had gone too far. A consignment was missing and unlike the "scallies" and halfwits they normally dealt with, the Colombians weren't likely to let it ride. Connor told them it had failed to arrive: they wanted proof, a "yellow pedal", a charge sheet from the authorities or a newspaper report proving the goods had been confiscated. Connor didn't have it. He blagged, said these things happen, and he would make it up to them on the next delivery. After all, the profits were huge. Everything was sorted he said, "all part of the deal". But in a warehouse on Liverpool's Canada Dock, a shipment of South American fish awaited delivery. It would wait a long time. For 300 kilos of the finest grade Colombian cocaine resided inside the tins. Michael knew because he had put it there. And he had a bad, bad feeling about the entire enterprise.

Somewhere above him a speaker announced the arrival of KL 1037. Michael rose and wandered down the Arrivals hall to wait outside Customs. Soon they began to appear. For the most part they were grim businessmen and heavy-eyed trippers returning home after a mid-week bender around the bars and fleshpots of Amsterdam. But one face was different. He was dark, his eyes hooded, and amongst the pale European complexions his stood out like a suntan on Blackpool pier. He ignored Michael but as he pushed through the line of waiting reps, an uncomfortable feeling settled in the pit of Michael's stomach. Michael tracked him all the way to the vestibule doors before returning his attention to those clearing the Blue Zone. Yet something niggled. He turned his head and saw that the stranger had stopped and was looking back at him. Their eyes locked.

They eyed each other up like gunfighters in the old West. Then the other smiled. From inside his mouth a gold incisor flashed and the hairs on Michael's neck bristled. He started towards him to find out what the fuck he was up to and had taken two steps when a tap on his shoulder made him stop.

"Michael Taylor?"

The voice pulled him round.

"I'm John Quiller."

Michael saw the outstretched hand. He hesitated then reached forward. The clasp was firm, the shake perfunctory. He released and shifted his gaze back to the doors. The stranger had gone.

Michael looked at Quiller. He wasn't what he was expecting. Small with round glasses and a neat, greying moustache, he looked like a professor away on vacation. Cardigan and brown tie beneath a grey mackintosh, and a felt fedora Michael guessed had cost more than what he was wearing, he looked small, lost in his clothes as if he was ill or recovering from cancer. But his eyes were clear and seemed to take in everything about him in an instant. He cleared his throat. "I'm to take you to Connor," he said. "He's looking forward to meeting you."

Quiller nodded and adjusted the small overnight bag on his shoulder.

Michael looked. "Is that all your luggage?"

Quiller grinned. "I travel light."

"But you have come from the States?"

"Four pm, New York, six am, Amsterdam." He looked at his watch. "Nine-thirty, Liverpool." Quiller pulled a face. "Transatlantic flight kills me."

Michael grinned sheepishly. "I wouldn't know."

Quiller raised an eyebrow. "You've never been to the States?" He pulled a lop-sided grin. "Lot of places to see, son, and so little time to do it in." He halted by the glass doors and looked out at the grey sky. "And they send me here."

Michael opened his mouth, was going to tell him it wasn't all bad, that Liverpool was one of the great cities of the world, but Quiller didn't wait and pushed out into the open.

A splatter of rain flew in their faces. Quiller grimaced. Michael glanced across and saw him holding down his hat. What the fuck was he expecting: blue skies and smiling faces?

Anyway, New York was just as shit. He had seen pictures on the TV. He shook his head and guided Quiller across the tarmac to the car park. Michael popped the locks on a blue Jag, waited while Quiller settled into the passenger seat and adjusted the belt. A minute later they were driving from the airport.

Quiller peered through the window. There wasn't much to see: newly constructed hotels, a few industrial units. He wiped his glasses with the end of his scarf and looked at Michael. "You've been with Connor some time?"

"A few years."

"That's good Michael. Some say loyalty has its own rewards." He replaced his glasses. "I prefer it in a bank account."

Michael said nothing.

Quiller pursed his lips as if unsure how to continue. "Connor's business, or the way he conducts his business, is of great interest to the people I represent."

Michael risked a glance away from the windscreen. "And?"

"You could do yourself a huge favour by being open with me."

"I'm not sure I understand?"

"Let's not kid ourselves Michael. I'm a broker, a go-between. I move in the same circles as certain other people. There's talk of a transaction going sour, of a missing product." He pulled a face. "To me it makes little difference one way or another. But my associates need to know whether doing business with Connor is a wise thing."

"You seem to know a lot about Connor already."

Quiller laughed. "And by inference you as well?" He turned his head back to the window. "Did you expect anything less?"

Michael didn't reply.

"Don't misunderstand, son. What we see is what we like. And what we see is a man of integrity. Your loyalty to Connor is admirable." Quiller smiled. "What d'you Brits say, 'you know where your bread's buttered'?"

Michael concentrated on negotiating a roundabout. Keeping his eyes on the road, he said, "I'm not sure what you want Mr Quiller. I'm just Connor's driver."

"Driver, lieutenant, confidant." Quiller shrugged. "Whatever Michael. But if you let him, Connor will drag you down."

Michael flushed. "As I said before, I'm just his driver."

Quiller nodded and settled himself into the seat. "As you say, Michael, as you say."

Michael took a sidelong glance at Quiller. Almost anonymous beneath his hat and coat, he could have been anyone; a favourite uncle perhaps. Yet there was something dark about him, something cold and calculating and Michael decided he would have to watch Mr Quiller very carefully.

They drove in silence until Michael turned off Speke Boulevard and headed towards Halewood and Connor's warehouse. It was situated on a sterile industrial site surrounded by box-like units of the same ilk. The delivery doors were open and as Michael pulled into the parking bay opposite, he saw Connor beneath the metal shutter. Wearing a white T-shirt that highlighted his biceps and faded tattoos, he was talking to a man in blue overalls. Making his point he squeezed the man's shoulder emphasising his orders then lifted his head. He saw the car. Grinning like a child who had just been given his favourite toy, Connor crossed the tarmac. He grabbed Quiller's hand as soon as he got out of the car. Their eyes locked. To Michael, watching, they looked like a couple of dogs sniffing each other's hindquarters. There was a brief moment as they stared each other out then Connor dropped Quiller's hand and ran it over his shaven head. He jerked a thumb behind him. "Let's go to the office. We can talk in private and I'll show you the business." He draped a friendly arm across Quiller's shoulders like they were long-lost buddies and guided him towards the building. Almost forgotten, Michael followed.

Inside wooden pallets and loose packaging littered the floor. Fluorescent strip-lights cast an artificial glow while, on shelving around the sides, boxed goods and small machine parts resided in haphazard disarray. It hardly looked professional but Connor swept an arm around his kingdom. "It don't look much but that's the beauty," he said and gave Quiller one of his trademark grins. "It's where I do my business."

Tucked to one side was the office. Connor opened the door and directed Quiller to a seat whilst he squeezed behind a table cluttered with books, diaries and ledgers. "And this is the hub." He patted the table and just caught a sheaf of papers as they began to slide towards the floor.

Standing with his back to the door, Michael raised his eyes.

Connor seemed not to realise that he was making himself look a clown. And in front of Quiller too. Connor had a big mouth that too often he let rule his head. Matched by an ego of equal proportion, he thought he could blag his way into or out of anything. In truth he was a small-time operator who had stumbled onto something big: making deals then ripping off his suppliers. After all, they were hardly able to go to the police. And Michael watched his back, had done so for years, ever since he had joined the "firm" and in that time he had learned to trust his instincts. And instinct told him not to trust Quiller. He rubbed his chin. Just how much did the little man know? Perhaps he had heard rumours and was merely fishing. But Michael didn't like it and more than once tried to get Connor's attention, tried to get him to slow down and take a break so that he could have a quiet word. But as usual Connor's mouth began to run away from him and he was in his element, playing The Big I Am, showing Quiller shipping manifestos and outlining his distribution network.

It was hopeless and as Connor and Quiller got down to business Michael's mind began to drift. He began to chase memories and dreams: memories of a simpler time before he got involved with Connor, and dreams of a future without him. He looked at him bending over the table, pouring over a map marked with red, green and blue lines.

All he had to do was....

A glass of Jameson's was thrust in his hand. Startled from his thoughts, he looked round the room. The meeting appeared to be over. Connor was standing next to him. He nudged him with his elbow, held his glass in the air and waited for Michael and Quiller to follow suit. "To new ventures," he said.

Michael swallowed it in one. He put the empty glass on the table and watched. To his amazement both men seemed satisfied. Connor laid his hand on Quiller's shoulder and began to guide him to the door.

"I've booked you a room at the Hard Day's Night." He opened his hands expansively. "It's the best hotel in Liverpool." He winked. "I got you the Lennon Suite," he said. "The piano," Connor nudged him with his elbow, "you know – the white one's there."

"God – really?"

"Michael will look after you. Anything you want," he said

and nodded towards

Michael. "You just ask my boy here." Connor winked – it was all part of the game and Michael played along. He could take the cheap jibes.

He moved behind Quiller and silently mouthed, 'We have to talk.'

Connor scowled. He turned back to Quiller. "And tonight we'll have a proper

Scouse night out." He patted him on the back. "Something you won't forget."

Outside the warehouse Connor turned Quiller aside and grasped his hand. "It's been good," he said. "Real good." He jerked a thumb behind. "Michael will take you to the hotel."

Lingering in the doorway, Michael saw them look back, and watched a frown cloud Quiller's face. His focus was somewhere behind and he twisted his head to see what had caught his attention. Breaking for lunch, Connor's warehouseman was sitting at a workbench. Scrutinising the newspaper in front of him, he was turning a key on a flat, silver tin.

Looking up, he saw three, staring faces. He paused and looked from one to the other. "What?"

Quiller looked at Connor.

Connor cleared his throat. "Sardines."

Quiller's brows shot up. "Ah," he said. "Fish," and he walked to the car.

Michael came and stood by Connor's shoulder. Before he could speak, Connor pushed a warning finger into Michael's face. "I don't want to hear it."

Michael shook his head. "This stinks."

"Don't spoil it." Connor put his mouth close to Michael's ear. "If this deal goes through we can walk away millionaires."

"I don't trust Quiller."

"He's just a go between, a courier for the big men. Remember if we get this right, you can keep Jan in shoes and handbags for the rest of her life." He squeezed Michael's arm. "But keep an eye on him." Connor shrugged. "Pays to be careful." He turned and went back to the warehouse.

Michael sucked his teeth. Okay, he would watch Quiller. And, like he always did, watch Connor's back.

*

Red was Connor's long-term retirement plan. Situated between the city's main-line station and principal hotel, it catered mostly to the city's guests. The girls were long-limbed, athletic and, for the most part, foreign – its clientele: bored businessmen, stag parties and groups of Irish boys on mad weekends of football and drink.

But tonight Connor had appropriated the club for himself.

He sprawled in a soft, leather armchair and drank champagne while his core of acolytes swarmed around him. From wall-mounted speakers music boomed while on the mirrored stage Latitia wrapped herself around a pole of polished gold. Cocoa brown, her skin glistened beneath the spotlights. For £10 she would grind away on your crotch – for £20 she would do it naked.

As guest of honour, Quiller sat next to Connor, laughed at his jokes and accepted Latitia's company when she had finished on stage. But he didn't fit in. He had changed clothes yet still wore a tie and shirt buttoned up to the neck. At his table near the back of the room, Michael sat alone, stayed sober and watched. And as he did he detected in Quiller a detached, remote air as if his mind were otherwise occupied. His champagne remained untouched, as did Latitia sitting at his side. So as the girls came from backstage and began to mix with Connor's crew and lines of coke appeared on the table tops, it came as no surprise when Quiller excused himself and came to sit at his table.

He whispered in Michael's ear then sat back.

Michael frowned. "Where?"

Quiller shrugged. "Anywhere – something Liverpool." He gazed around Connor's club and shook his head. "This could be New York or Chicago." He shrugged. "Different city, same scene."

"What is it you want?"

He made a small, helpless movement with his hands. "I don't know. An English pub with English beer." He waved his hands. "I've seen all this before."

Michael pursed his lips. What harm could it do? And Connor had told him to keep a close eye on him. "Okay," he said, "I know a few places." He got up from the table. "I'll tell Connor

144

we're leaving."

Quiller caught Michael's wrist. "Leave him with the girls. He'll feel obliged to come and I don't want to spoil the party."

Michael looked at Quiller, met his smiling eyes and remembered his first impression. What did he truly want? He didn't know, but maybe this was a way to find out. Quiller was a long way from home. What could happen? He tilted his head and led Quiller to the foyer.

The city throbbed with life. Outside Red, a sea of noise greeted them. Taxis choked the roads, crowds clogged the pavements and from open pub doorways laughter and music leached into the night. The weekend had started, and Liverpool knew how to party.

Michael took Quiller to the Fly for the beer, Smokie's for the fun and the

Liffey for the craic. And Quiller liked the craic.

Scruffy and frayed around the edge, the Liffey's heart was emerald green. A wooden floor, frosted-glass windows and imitation gas lamps gave it a sombre, Dickensian feel. But if in the afternoons the Liffey's custom revolved around old men and the racing channel, the nights were different: karaoke and live music packed the place out. Tonight was no exception. On a raised dais at the back of the pub, a trio of musicians were playing Irish standards to a captive audience. In an area free from tables, patrons with sweat-licked faces sang and danced, cheered at the end of every tune and hoped that tonight would be different – that they wouldn't be going home alone.

Quiller insisted on buying the drinks. He pushed his way through the crowd at the bar and joined Michael at his table. He set the drinks down, Caffrey's for Michael, Guinness for him, and sat opposite. Almost immediately the band announced a break. He threw up his hands. "Hey what's this? Soon as we come in they stop playing?"

Michael sipped his beer. "They won't stop for long," he said and shook his head.

It was the same every Friday – the same music, the same tunes. You could set your watch each time they played "The Wild Rover". "They never stop for long," he added.

Quiller loosened his tie and stared at Michael. "Thought anymore about this morning's conversation?"

Michael didn't answer.

Quiller frowned. "What is it about Connor? What endears him to you so much?"

Michael looked, rolled beer around his mouth and slowly swallowed. "It's like this," he said. "I'd just left the army, we had a kid on the way and I was working the doors for a couple of clubs in town. It was that or working in Asda on Smithdown Road." Michael shrugged. "Connor gave me an alternative, a way out."

Quiller leaned forward. "Whatever it is you owe Connor, or think you owe, has been repaid." He picked up his glass and tilted it towards him. "You're the one who takes the risks Michael. Have you thought about your wife and child if something were to happen?"

"They'll be okay."

"No financial worries, eh?"

Michael's eyes darted back to Quiller. The guy was relentless. Deliberately he repeated, "They'll be okay."

For a moment they stared into each other's eyes. Michael waited while Quiller sat back and tapped his lip. Finally he made up his mind, for he nodded and gestured Michael close. Even amidst the music and voices he didn't want to be overheard. "Let's quit playing. Connor's operation is impressive but he's a liability. My associates need a distribution network and with your connections you could head it." He jabbed Michael with his finger. "I could recommend it. No more risks Michael – that's for other guys. You just sit back and count the profits."

"What about Connor."

Quiller shrugged. "Connor's a tool. He's made enemies with people who take a line to being ripped off."

"And me?"

"You were a loyal foot soldier doing what he was told."

Michael stared over the room.

"I can square it. C'mon Michael. What d'you say?"

Michael looked at the people around him: ordinary, everyday folk whose only wish was for beer and a laugh. In truth he was one of those people. And Quiller was offering him everything. He picked up his glass and thought about Jan and the baby. And then he smiled, for he had everything already.

"Like I said before, Mr Quiller, I'm just Connor's driver."

He took a long, deep drink.

"Final word?"

Michael nodded. "Final word."

"That's a shame Michael, a damn shame." He shook his head. "You see, one way or another, I have to find out." The little man had suddenly become very serious. He stared at Michael. Behind the round glasses his gaze never wavered.

Michael's laugh was dry. "And how d'you mean to do that?" he said and moved forward so he was in Quiller's face. "Remember, you're in my city." He took another mouthful of beer and sat back, matching Quiller's gaze with one of equal intensity. Michael's face changed. He looked at the remains of drink in his glass and licked his lips. It was only his third – or was it his fourth? He put the glass down and rubbed his temples. Something was wrong. His vision began to waver.

"Strong beer, eh Michael?"

Shit. He tried to stand but his legs were weak, he couldn't feel them and he collapsed back on the seat. He made a feeble attempt to grab Quiller then put a hand to his head. Michael gazed around the room. Faces turned to look and as he tried to focus upon them they distorted and blurred. He was going to be sick.

From a great distance away he heard Quiller's voice. "It's all right folks, just a little too much beer. As he started to slide beneath the table, a big hand caught his shoulder and stopped him. It was the last thing he remembered.

*

Michael shook his head. He must have passed out. He took a deep breath and began to cough as cold air rasped into his lungs.

The cellar was deserted.

Without thinking, he pulled at the ties binding his wrists. He stopped and tried again. A spark of hope flashed. They didn't feel as tight, loose even. Hardly able to believe his luck, he began to work his hands, pulling and straining, twisting one way and then another until he had widened the opening and could slip one from the plastic loop. At last they were free. He breathed a sigh of relief.

Seconds later a sickening burst of clarity brought home the

truth of his situation.

He had to find Connor. Everything he held dear depended on it. With ice-cold fingers he untied his ankles and looked around. His clothes lay in a heap on the floor. He dressed quickly and checked his pockets. Wallet and phone had gone but they had left his keys. Legs stiff and barely working, Michael staggered to the door. Listening for any sign of life beyond, he carefully pushed it open. Beyond was a small passage; a few metres to his left a flight of stairs led upwards. The place was derelict, broken timber and fallen plaster littered the floor. The stairs were bare. He trod softly, one step at a time, holding his breath each time he heard a creak until he reached the top and another closed door. Time was critical. It was shit or bust. Gathering the last of his strength, Michael kicked the door back and rushed forward ready to meet any opposition with his fists. He needn't have worried; the place was as deserted as the cellar. A pent-up breath escaped and he winced as pain racked his body. A rib, maybe two, were broken. It didn't matter, he had other concerns. Michael looked around, saw upturned tables and mouldy walls, a bar that hadn't been used in years, and guessed he was in some abandoned city pub. Outside he could hear traffic. The windows had been tinned over, but one of the covers had been pushed aside and leaked light. Putting his hands beneath the metal frame, he pulled it aside and climbed out.

Sunlight hit him. Blinded by the rays, he stepped off the kerb into the road. A horn blared, a taxi swerved and as it passed the driver gave him the finger. Michael moved back into the crowd. As the lights changed he was swept along. Half way across he realised he was going in the wrong direction. He turned and pushed his way through a tide of jostling bodies. He was a mess – he saw it in the faces of the people passing: crumpled clothes and bloody nose, but he didn't care. Ignoring their stares, he began to run.

Michael had once run for the army at the inter-service games at Halton, but that was a long time ago. Convulsed in coughs, he held onto a lamppost – gasping, panting, sucking air into his lungs as if his life depended on it. No more smoking he promised – ever – and he took one more deep breath and started over. There was no alternative, he had to cross that line.

The car was parked in a side street behind the station. He

turned the corner and walked the final yards, wiping his face with his sleeve and brushing his sweat-licked fringe out of his eyes. He popped the locks and collapsed on the driver's seat. Just for a moment, he allowed himself to rest. He closed his eyes and began to drift. Something niggled: a thought, his consciousness – whatever it was he was grateful, for his eyes sprung open. Furious with himself, he beat his hands against the steering wheel. He had to stay in control. Michael pulled open the glove box. Inside was a Browning automatic. He checked the magazine, racked the slide and pushed it into the waistband of his trousers. He checked the clock on the dash: 9.30. Connor would be at the gym.

In normal circumstances Michael kept to the speed limits lest he draw unwanted attention. Today it didn't matter. Ignoring red lights, he flashed past cars and headed towards an area of renovated dockland near the river. Connor's gym stood on reclaimed ground. It was a modern, flat-roofed building surrounded by used-car lots and reconditioned warehouses. The membership was exclusive, the fees exorbitant. Connor liked it that way.

Michael hardly slowed as he negotiated the roundabout. He flew through the car park narrowly missing a Ford Focus coming the other way and hit the brakes. He slid to a halt in front of the double glass doors. Placing his head on the steering wheel, he forced himself to breathe slow and even. A moment later he raised his eyes, and met those of Connor. He was staring at him.

Emerging from the gym just as Michael approached, he had heard the screech of tyres and stopped. As Michael got out of the car, his face hardened. Shifting his sports holdall from right to left hand, he jabbed an accusing finger at him. "Jan's gonna kill you," he said. "She's been on the phone all night wondering where you're at." He shook his head in disgust at his friend's behaviour. "She didn't give up till three." He let the message sink in then his face split a huge grin. "Don't worry," he said. "I covered for you." Connor looked round then jerked his head forward as if he were imparting a secret. "Said you were entertaining a client." His laughter died when he saw the gun in Michael's hand.

Michael held the Browning steady. His eyes moved only slightly when Quiller stepped from the back of a parked BMW.

He refocused on Connor and gave him a small, apologetic shrug. "Sorry, Connor," he said, "but I have no choice."

Connor dropped the holdall and tried to step back inside the gym.

Michael fired twice. The first passed through the palm of Connor's outstretched hand and hit him in the face. It slowed the bullet enough so that it didn't kill him. The second did. It entered below his left eye and exited the back of his head taking five inches of skull with it. Connor was dead before he hit the ground.

As the echo from the shots faded, someone screamed. Inside the gym, people scattered for cover, phones were sought, numbers punched in and the police called. But Michael didn't move. He was watching the blood pool around Connor's head. Only when he heard the thump of small fists on glass was the spell broken. He swivelled his head. Inside the Beemer, Emily had her face pressed against the window. She was sobbing. Her blonde hair swished side to side as her tiny hands pounded the windscreen. Beside her, the driver leaned forward and pulled her back into the seat. He caught Michael's eye and grinned. A gold incisor glinted in his open mouth.

Quiller sidled up to him. He looked at the lifeless body of Connor and pushed it with his foot. "Well that's the first part of our deal, Michael," he said and his mouth twitched. "The rest is up to you." He walked back to the BMW and got in the back seat.

Michael took a deep breath and glanced once more at the car and the little girl he would never again see.

It wasn't that hard.

He tore his eyes from Emily's face and put the barrel of the gun inside his mouth.

No he thought – it wasn't that hard at all.

Sullivan's Steps

They wore the uniform of the street, black hooded jackets and baggie tracksuit bottoms that merged with the night. Against the backdrop of gloomy terraced housing, they basked in an aura of menace.

Sullivan had seen them before they even knew he was there. One leaned against the wall. He had a dog lead in his fist and a Staffordshire bull terrier at his feet. Another lounged idly by. But Sullivan's eyes were drawn to the third. He stood on the kerb, aloof, self-contained; happy in his own skin. Sullivan's gaze lingered on the tall, thin youth. There was something about him, the way he held himself perhaps, that aroused in Sullivan a vague recognition that this was he thirty years before. In those days, keeping a distance between himself and his friends had been as much about pride as it had survival.

Only one man had he truly trusted. And that was one too many.

A whistle, two short, one long, came from the dark behind him. Sullivan saw the looks, the exchange of glances. The boy by the kerb pulled the peak of his baseball cap lower, moved to block his progress. As Sullivan drew level the one with the dog took a cigarette from his mouth. "What's in the bag mate?"

Sullivan ignored the call, shifted his holdall from right to left hand, and side-stepped the boy on the pavement. From the corner of his eye he saw the flash of contempt. The one with the dog scraped himself off the wall.

"Hey, you lanky streak of piss."

Sullivan stopped, turned, flicked his eyes over the three boys. Watched a fourth run to join them. They stood in a loose half circle across the pavement and onto the road. There was strength in their unity, comfort in their closeness. Something else too. An air of anticipation tinged the air. Sullivan could almost smell it.

The boy with the dog stepped forward, jerked the lead. Brought to life, the little dog snarled and snapped. As it leapt towards Sullivan, the boy yanked back on the lead, choked its growls. Again he gave it slack. Bounding forward, he did the same. Tormented, the dog slavered in excitement.

The boy shook his head as if a mistake of utmost gravity had been performed.

"Don't walk through here like you own the fucking place, la." A chorus of approval followed.

Sullivan said nothing. He looked at the boys, searched their eyes one by one, showed he wasn't to be intimidated.

One joined the boy with the dog. "He's fronting you, Macca."

"Yeah?"

"Yeah. Look at him."

Macca's face changed as a torrent of rage swept through him. Crouched over his dog, holding it back by its leather harness, he raised his eyes. They met those of David Sullivan. And in the moment it took to realise he'd made one huge mistake, Macca slipped the leash.

Sullivan had faced dogs before. Big dogs, dogs kept to guard their owner's property and deter the casual thief: there had been that pair of Alsatians in Hitchens transport yard all those years before. Yet the power of the little dog shocked him. All he saw was a square head and jaws full of teeth. As it leapt towards him, he just had time to swing the holdall down before it bit his arm. Instead it clamped onto the bag.

The dog's neck muscles bulged, almost tore the bag from his hand. Ignoring the howls of encouragement from the boys, Sullivan looked into the beast's black eyes. Maybe it saw something of its own nature in the creature standing over it, for it paused. But dumb animals know only so much and a moment later, it began again. Breath gurgled and rasped in its throat as it shook its head side to side, trying to wrest the bag from Sullivan's hand. But he was ready this time. Sullivan took a deep breath and began to lift the bag. The Staffie's legs slipped and, refusing to relinquish its hold, it rose with it. Sullivan aimed a kick at the white blaze in its chest. There was a solid thud, the beast fell away, shook itself then came again.

Sullivan misjudged its jaws.

A dozen tiny daggers in a vice of steel, broke the skin of his arm. Sullivan grimaced, dropped the holdall. There was no pain, not yet, but knew it would come. He also had a measure of the dog's strength and could gauge its power. With the Staff still clamped firmly on his arm, Sullivan slipped his free hand into his back pocket, drew his knife, and thumbed the blade.

Macca saw the steel in Sullivan's hand, screamed, "Don't you dare, don't you fucking dare."

Gritting his teeth, Sullivan raised his arm. As the Staffie's head rose, Sullivan pushed the knife into its throat. When he felt the resistance of the windpipe he pushed harder, felt the warm air from its lungs. It was as if a light had been switched off, the dog's eyes dulled. As he pulled the blade, blood followed, the pressure on his wrist lessened, and he used the blade to lever the dog's jaw off his arm. It fell to the floor, twitched then lay still in a pool of its own blood. It was enough. Situation over. But like his dog, Macca didn't know when to let go.

"You bastard, you fucking bastard." He jabbed a finger, advanced on Sullivan, his rage burning like wild fire. "That was mine. My fucking property." Unsure of themselves, his crew of three shuffled behind.

Sullivan waited until the boy was close then brought the knife to his throat. Held it there. And in that instant Macca knew, had no doubt whatsoever, that if he moved, this man would have no compunction about ripping open his throat and stamping him into the ground. No one breathed.

Sullivan was easy, knew this could go either way, and was ready. Sensing movement, he switched focus. It was the boy with the baseball cap, the one he marked out earlier as the one to watch. He braced himself but the boy moved slowly, without malice. He reached out, put a hand on Macca's shoulder, slowly eased him back to the fold. Sullivan looked into his narrow eyes, saw an understanding of the way things were. Flicked his eyes once more over Macca. The fight had left him.

Keeping his eyes on the boys, Sullivan folded his blade and picked up his holdall.

Turning his back, he walked away, didn't look again. Knew he didn't have to.

*

The corner café was much as Sullivan remembered. Though a new name hung over the door and blue checked tablecloths adorned the tables, the tea still came in mugs, they still served all-day breakfasts, and the daily special was still a bowl of

Scouse. The place had changed for the better and he said so to the girl behind the counter.

She held his gaze for the briefest moment. "Yeah," she said, "it doesn't smell of old men and piss anymore."

Now that, supposed Sullivan, was a good thing, and he took his breakfast to a table where he could look out of the window.

Outside, the rush hour traffic was easing. Sullivan settled in, spread a newspaper, began to read. He was barely past the headlines when the door opened and a face from the past stood in the doorway. Though older, Pixie's gaunt, emaciated figure was as familiar as ever. Sullivan jerked his head, called him over.

"Heard you was back," said Pixie, a wide, gap-tooted grin spread over his face.

"News travels fast."

He nodded at Sullivan's wrist where a thin layer of gauze and lint peeped out from beneath his sleeve. "Well, sticking Johnny Mac's dog is a bit like putting an advert in the Echo."

"Johnny Mac?" Sullivan pulled the cuff over the offending bandage. "Bobby's lad?"

"That's him."

"Bobby still around then?"

Pixie's face darkened. "Yeah, he's still around."

Sullivan nodded, went back to his paper. Pixie waited, shifted his weight from one foot to the other until Sullivan pushed out a chair. "Sit down Pix, you make the place look untidy."

Pixie took off his hat, slid into the seat opposite, pointed to the plate on the table.

"You eating that?"

Sullivan looked at the toast. Shook his head. "Fill your boots lad."

Pixie rubbed his fingers. "Ta Sul." He teased a piece from the bottom, inspected the thick layer of butter, took a bite. "That why you're back then?"

Sullivan's brows knitted.

"Bobby Mac." Pixie wiped the grease from his chin. "No one would blame you.

Not after what he done, like."

"Long time ago, Pix."

"Some things take their time. Heard you say that once."

Sullivan went back to his paper. "Through the years I've learned things that once seemed important eventually mean very little." He licked a thumb, turned a page.

Pixie stopped chewing, pulled a face Sullivan never saw. Wasn't quite sure what he was hearing. He waited for Sullivan to elaborate. He didn't, so he took another slice of toast.

The café quietened. Apart from Sullivan, Pixie and the waitress, the place was deserted.

Pixie picked at his food. "So," he said, "what does bring you back?"

Sullivan ran a finger over his moustache. "Wanted to see the place again."

"That all?"

"That's all. Want to see what's changed."

"Frigging hell, Sul, have you seen the city? Hotels, shops," he spread his arms, "all sorts of shit."

"I mean around here."

"Nothing new here, Sul. The only thing we've got more of is funeral homes."

"What about the people? Bobby Mac for instance?"

"No difference there Sul."

"And the office?"

"Still Black's."

Sullivan lifted his tea, gazed over Pixie's shoulder.

For a little while neither spoke. Eventually Pixie broke the silence. "I've got me own place now," he said.

"Yours?"

"Rent." Concentrating on the table, he began to crush sugar granules with the back of his nail. "Live with Maureen Fallon."

"Sandra's sister?"

"That's right."

"Bloody hell Pix, she's just a kid."

"Was, Sul. It's seventeen years since you was here. She's all grown up."

"It's sixteen actually. But point taken." He was silent for a moment. "And Sandra?"

Pixie wiped his hands on the tablecloth. "Like I said, things don't change." He shrugged. "Where else would she go?"

"How d'you mean?"

"Don't you know?"

Sullivan shrugged.

"After you went down she took up with Bobby Mac."

"Tell me something I don't know, Pix."

"After that, I mean. He met some tart singing in a club and dropped her like a stone. Left her with a kid and a bad habit."

Sullivan pursed his lips. Some things were better left in the past.

Pixie opened his mouth but something in Sullivan's face warned him to keep it shut. He looked at the table until his mouth got the better of him. "So you've not come for anything special then?"

"No."

They stared at each other until Pixie sniffed. "Gotta go," he said and slid from the table. As he laid a hand on the door he paused and looked back. "Sandra still drinks in the Eastern, you know."

Sullivan looked up.

"She'll be there tonight."

Sullivan opened his mouth but before he could reply the door closed and Pixie was gone.

*

Pixie didn't stop until he passed the parade of shops. Making sure Sullivan hadn't followed, he fished phone from pocket, and made the call. It was answered immediately.

"He's not saying," said Pixie. "Yeah, course I tried. All he's saying is that he's come to see what's new." He nodded to the voice at the other end. "That's all – honest." Pixie frowned. "Will he be there? Told him Sandra goes every Thursday." He smiled. "Don't worry. He'll be there." He nodded again. "Yeah, thanks Bobby."

The call ended and Pixie blew a sigh of relief. Obligation completed. He deleted the number, walked away. And as he did, he tried his very best to forget all about David friggin' Sullivan.

*

Sandra Fallon wasn't a kid anymore, but as she walked through the door of the Great Eastern, she could almost believe she was a teenager again. He was there, just like he always used to be there, and sixteen years passed in the blink of an eye. The bad years, the dot years, the ones that weren't so bad but weren't so very good either. But every year was cursed with the memory of David bloody Sullivan.

Dressed in a casual two-piece suit and Italian leather shoes, he sat at the bar; and she had to admit, he still looked pretty good. Sandra took a deep breath and walked over.

The Eastern was a communal, tight little pub and there were fewer than a dozen people there. But as she slipped between the tables and headed to where he sat, she was acutely aware they all knew her and Dave's long history. She stood next to him, almost brushed his elbow. "The fuck you doing here?"

He looked at her. "Was going to ask you that."

"I live here."

"So you do." He beckoned the barman. "Drink?"

"Vodka coke."

Sullivan laughed.

"What's funny?"

"Just something Pixie said."

"That little shit."

"What you got against him?"

"He's taken up with our Maureen."

Sullivan shrugged. "She's a big girl. So I heard."

"He's a fucking druggie." Sandra lowered her voice. "Deals as well. That's how he can afford the rent."

Sullivan laid a hand on hers. "You do what you have to, San. You know that." Surprised to find her hand staying longer than it should, she pulled it free, cleared her throat. Sullivan handed a note over the bar. "Your hair's different."

She choked back a laugh. "Should think so after seventeen years."

"It suits you."

She ran a hand through the blonde streaks, accepting his awkward compliment, and pulled up a stool. "It hides the grey," she said and looked at Sullivan's black, very black, hair. "See you do the same." She pushed her tongue between her teeth.

The lines around his eyes creased. "Sandra," he said, "leave me my one vanity, please."

She pulled a face. "Sorry Dave."

For a little while they sat in silence. Sullivan took large mouthfuls of lager, gassy and tasteless compared to what he was used to, while Sandra sipped at her vodka. The TV, the clack of balls from the pool table in the back room and the subdued talk of others filled the void.

"What are you doing here Dave?"

Sullivan lifted his pint in the air and gazed at the contents. "Well it's not for the beer, that's for sure."

She laughed and looked down at her hands. "Heard you went to Spain."

He nodded. "I have an apartment in Valencia."

"Don't miss this place then?"

"Not till now."

Just like it used to, Sandra's stomach twisted. She looked at her drink, swirled the contents around the base. "I'm serious Dave, why have you come back?"

"Like I keep telling everyone, I needed to. Just wanted to see the place again.

Maybe make my peace." There was a catch in his voice, and Sandra felt he was about to say more. But he stopped himself, took another drink.

Sandra pushed. "But why now?"

Sullivan ordered more drinks. It was a gesture designed to end the conversation and for a while it did. Behind the bar, the guy turned the TV off and slotted a CD in the machine: Motown classics. Soon the opening riff of "My Girl" drifted through the bar.

Sandra shifted in her seat. "Never thought I'd see you again."

"Did you want to?"

"Ten years is a long time."

"It is when all you see is four walls."

"I tried Dave, I really did."

"But you had a better offer."

"Don't say it like that. I had my reasons."

"Like?"

"I was pregnant."

The words stung like they were cut with acid.

"Your kid, Dave."

Sullivan shook himself. "You're full of shit, Sandra. D'you

know that?" He turned his back, reached for his beer.

Sandra felt the heat rise to her face. "Go fuck yourself, Dave."

He didn't even look at her.

She got off the stool, moved round so she could push her face into his. "Did you really expect me to sit on my arse for ten years waiting for you?"

"Ten minutes would have been nice."

Sandra opened her mouth. Years of frustration filled her mouth with the bile of rage. And it was there, all there, ready to fall like an avalanche. She gripped herself, forced herself to calm down. She took a deep breath. "Same old Dave, eh?" She picked her bag off the bar. "Thanks for the drink." She pushed herself away, stopped. "His name's Christopher," she said and took another step. "If you want to know, that is." She turned abruptly and walked through the door.

*

Outside, Sandra leant against the wall and closed her eyes. Hadn't wanted it to be like that, hadn't meant to feel anything. Didn't want to. She fumbled in her pocket for cigarettes and stuck one between her lips. It took a couple of strikes of the lighter before the flame caught. She looked at her hand. It was shaking. She inhaled, let the smoke drift from her mouth.

"Well?" The voice startled her. Bobby Mac stepped from the shadows.

Sandra took another drag of her cigarette, shook her head. "Nothing. He's just sitting there like he owns the fucking place."

Bobby's shoulder twitched. "It was just a thought."

"I tried didn't I?"

"You get nothing for trying girl."

"Come on Bobby." Her voice softened. "If I say I tried…"

Bobby grunted. He put his hand in his pocket and pulled out a small, clear packet.

A residue of white powder lay at the bottom. "Ought not to give you this."

Sandra forced a laugh. "You know me, Bobby."

"Yeah, I know you." He tossed the packet into Sandra's hands, watched it disappear into her pocket.

"Ta Bobby. She breathed a sigh of relief. "You coming round tonight?"

Bobby's small eyes gave nothing away. "Maybe."

She hesitated, unsure what to do, then began to walk. After a few paces she stopped.

"What now?"

Bobby Mac laid a hand on his neck and began to knead the muscles. "Guess I'll have to ask him myself."

*

Sullivan lifted the glass to his lips and cursed himself for a fool. Sandra Fallon. He had loved her once – thought he had anyway. That was before the judge said ten years and she ran into the arms of Bobby Mac before he was even taken down to the cells. His face darkened. Pregnant. The fuck was she trying to pull? He shook his head, caught his reflection in the line of beer pumps: elongated and distorted, just like his reputation. And as he looked, there was another, staring back at him until their features merged and he couldn't tell one from the other.

"Hello, Dave."

Bobby Mac slid onto the barstool at Sullivan's side. There were others too, nearby, closing around him. People were finishing their drinks and moving away, fast. He swivelled his head. "Bobby."

Bobby hit him twice. Short, savage jabs to his kidneys. Sullivan's breath exploded from his lungs as fell across the bar. Still thinking, he reached for his glass but before he could break it against Bobby's head, it was knocked from his hand. A blow from the side felled him and he crashed to the floor.

Sullivan shook his head, tried to clear his vision. He knew the score, had taken hidings before, and against three it was usually damage limitation. Even so if he could just...

He twisted quickly, thrust out a hand, tried to grab an ankle and bring Bobby down. A kick in his chest forced him to reassess. He rolled onto his side and was kicked again. A rib, maybe two, cracked. He coughed, spat blood. Blows rained down and for a while he may have lost conscious. Thinking on it afterwards, would have been glad if he had.

Pushed, rolled, then half carried, Sullivan felt the cool night breeze on his face before he was tossed in the air like unwanted garbage. He landed heavily, the hard concrete tearing breath from body. A security light flipped on. Down amongst the empty kegs, broken bottles and rubbish of the Great Eastern's back yard, Sullivan clung to a semblance of life that had nothing to do with what his brain was telling him. He heard the crunch of glass beneath a heavy foot and braced himself for more. But they stopped and a familiar voice whispered close to his ear.

"Don't know why you're here Dave. Don't care either. But we don't want you – ever."

Even in his pain Sullivan tried to smile. "We?"

Bobby Mac stood up. "You're a dinosaur, Dave. People see you, they get reminded of the past. A past we've spent years trying to forget. You don't belong anymore."

Through the numbness of his body, Sullivan felt the foot push his face. He didn't move, couldn't. Even so he heard the voice and footsteps as they faded away. And the last parting shot. "Go home Dave. Go home and don't come back."

After what seemed an age, Sullivan started to move. Slowly, very slowly, he climbed to his knees, patted his face, checked his teeth. Sullivan looked around the debris and rubbish. Go home, said Bobby, and he couldn't help the smile spreading on his face until the pain got too much. Home he thought. Why, he was already there.

*

Bobby Mac stood in the door-well of Black's and watched cars – and people. In fact he watched everything that moved, every shadow that crept through the night. Sullivan hadn't been seen for six long weeks. And every day longer was a shortening of the fuse that led to his brain.

"Got a light?"

Sandra's voice made him jump. She was standing behind him, unlit cigarette in her hand. He rummaged in his pocket, found his Zippo, flipped the lid. His hand had the slightest tremor. As she took the flame, Sandra glanced at the lighter. "Didn't Dave give you that?"

Bobby Mac rubbed his thumb over the worn nameplate. "I guess." He put it back in his pocket.

They smoked in silence until Sandra said, "He's not coming."

But Bobby shook his head. "It's not like him. He was never one to take a hiding.

He'd nurse it, play with it, roll it around in his head until he was ready."

"And then?"

Bobby said nothing.

Sandra shrugged. "Well you should know. You were like brothers once." She hesitated. "You never told me Bobby, why did you give him up?"

"Did what I had to." He looked away, dashed the cigarette to the floor. Stamped on it. "Shit. Should have finished him. Should have finished him when I had the chance."

"But you didn't. Now you're like a man with an itch you can't scratch." She reached out, touched his arm. "If he was still around you would have heard." She waved her cigarette. "He'll have gone back to Spain, tail between his legs."

A car turned, headed towards them and Bobby Mac's head flicked up, eyes following it along the road until it passed clear.

A tired breath escaped Sandra's mouth. "Coming back inside?"

Bobby lit another cigarette. "Finish this first."

"Suit yourself." She pushed at the door and for a brief moment Bobby heard laughter and music, escape from reality. But the door closed behind her and he was left with the night, and his own dark thoughts.

*

Inside it was busy. Friday's always produced a mixture of punters. Some having a couple before heading into town and those staying local, making a night of it. It made for a good, heady atmosphere. Lager, 2-4-1 doubles, bottles of Bud and Brown Mixed were passed over the bar and drunk with the abandon of those who knew the weekend had already started. And started it had. Couples and groups dotted the tables, but most hung around the bar, talking over the music, waiting for the karaoke.

Bobby smoked another three cigarettes before he went back

inside. He walked around the bar, side-stepped the overspill and squeezed past a group of women. Sandra was talking to a younger guy. Bobby smiled to himself. Guessed the boy had more money than sense. At the end of the bar, a pint of Guinness waited. He climbed onto his stool and nodded to his boys sitting at a table beside the Gents. PB and Scott weren't renowned for their intellect, but they supplied the suitable muscle a man like Bobby Mac was expected to have. He raised his glass, looked over the bar. It was a good crowd tonight, banter flew back and forth. Yet he knew it could turn. A wrong look or a bad word, perceived slights and pretensions of valour and it could kick off in an instant. Bobby had seen it all, knew violence could escalate in the blink of an eye. That's why he liked to be there, hands on. Knew how to kill it dead.

A round of catcalls broke his thoughts. A short girl with frizzled hair and permanent tan was taking the mic for the first song. Bobby knew her mother. Just like her, Dee Lane had a good voice. He swivelled round on his stool to watch. Her voice was light but she had a power and resonance that swelled on the big notes. Talk was she had auditioned for The X Factor. Bobby turned back to his drink. Give it a year or two and she'd have a kid and be working in Tesco.

He paused with the glass halfway to his lips. A stranger had pushed his way to the bar. Side-faced, all Bobby saw was an unkempt beard and greasy, shoulder length hair. He wore a stockman's coat and black leather biker boots. Must have snuck in when everyone's attention was focused on Dee. Not the sort Bobby wanted in his bar. He glanced at PB and Scott. Too busy watching the girls, paying little attention to what was going on. Craning his neck and leaning forward to get a better view, Bobby's eyes widened. For at that moment the stranger turned and faced him. Bobby Mac froze. Though his beard obscured half his face, the rest of his features were unmistakable. Bobby moved, knew he had to be quick. For the past few weeks he'd kept a snub-nosed Smith and Wesson in his jacket pocket for just such an occasion. But even as he went for it, already knew it was too late.

*

Sullivan held Bobby Mac's gaze, watched his hand slip into his right-hand pocket, saw the glint of steel. But he was slow, much too slow. Leaning on the bar, Sullivan's left hand already gripped the stock, finger resting on the trigger guard, of the over-and-under shotgun hidden inside his coat. A foot of barrel had been sawn off. In one movement he pulled the gun, wedged it against his hip, and pointed it at Bobby. It took a moment for those around to see, to realise what they were witnessing. Then the panic began. A scream, latched onto by others, echoed around the room. People looked, saw, fell over each other in their rush to escape.

The scene was surreal, Sullivan felt the master of time, his thoughts and actions so much quicker than anyone else's. Bobby Mac's, at least. He smiled, enjoyed the sensation. Then he pulled the trigger.

The explosion ripped the heart from the bar. Those who hadn't seen, those who didn't understand, began to scream and join the rush for the exits. Tables fell, glasses smashed. Sullivan ignored the chaos, watched Bobby. Watched him spin on his seat and grip his belly. Not before he saw him hit the floor did he turn the other barrel on the table with the goons. He fired. Shards of wood flew into the air peppering the men at its side. The table collapsed taking PB and Scott to the floor. He broke the gun. Ejectors threw out the spent cartridges and he replaced them with two more from his pocket. Sighting along the barrel, he waited until one of them raised his head. Big mistake. Sullivan's shoulder jerked as he squeezed the shotgun's trigger. The top of the table disintegrated. So did PB's head. Sullivan walked forward, peered over its broken frame. Bleeding from a dozen wounds, wood chips splintering his face, Scott scrabbled in the debris for his automatic. Sullivan got close – real close – and squeezed the trigger. He turned slowly. The bar was empty. Everyone had gone. Everyone except Bobby Mac.

*

Bobby Mac twitched. In the panic following the first shot, he had lain amongst the stampeding legs, unable to move. Once, only once, had someone bent down and looked. Grateful, he tried to speak but Pixie's face broke into a wide, gap-toothed grin, then he calmly lifted his wallet from inside his jacket and ran like fuck. Bastard.

Bobby tried to reach for his gun but his right arm wouldn't move. In fact he could feel nothing on that side of his body. Curious, too, about the wetness spreading between his legs, he hoped he hadn't pissed himself.

Somewhere in the empty room, a glass rolled off a table. Bobby strained, tried to hear what else. He heard footsteps, footsteps closing. And he heard the unmistakable sound of a breaking shotgun, its cartridges bouncing on the floor. Lastly he heard the snap of metal as the piece was readied for action. Bobby Mac closed his eyes, knew what was coming. Prayed for it to be quick. But Sullivan wasn't that kind of man. The kiss of metal on his cheek forced his eyes open. He looked. At the other end of the barrel, Sullivan stared down into his face. Bobby squeezed a shallow breath between his lips. "Why?"

"Couldn't let you shaft me again, Bobby. Thought I was over it, thought I could walk away." He shrugged, "Guess I was wrong."

Bobby shook his head.

"You mean why I came back?" Sullivan took a deep breath. "Wanted to see the place,

Bobby. That's all. God's honest truth. Saw a doctor not long back." He shrugged. "Gave me a year, maybe two if I behaved myself." Sullivan checked himself, looked over the room. Bobby saw the shade of a smile. "Was going well until tonight."

When he returned his attention to Bobby, there was a sadness in his eyes, but whether regret or revenge Bobby didn't know. It made little difference. "Man gets a different perspective when he knows he's going to die." The smile had gone. "Isn't that right, Bobby?"

Bobby tried to speak, to get the last word in just as he always used to. All he managed was a grimace that may have been a smile.

"Good," said Sullivan and he pushed the barrels hard into Bobby Mac's head.

"I'm glad we agree."

Then everything went black.

*

Sandra had run before the first shot had been fired. She knew Sullivan better than anyone and when she saw him at the bar, had left by the nearest door. She heard the shots, saw the stampede and now, compelled by something she did not understand, stood on the corner staring at Black's.

She was in the process of lighting a cigarette when two figures ran to a line of parked cars. Crouching behind a Cavalier, they took turns watching the door.

Sandra's stomach churned. She hesitated then started towards them. Laying a hand on the boot, she peered round. "Chris?"

She saw him, saw the gun in his hand, and the look on his face; calm and sure just like his dad used to be. The other one, Macca, hissed at her to go but Sandra ignored him, laid a hand on his arm. "Don't do this."

"I have to."

"No you don't. Don't listen to him." She hesitated. "There's something you have to know."

But it was too late because Macca's voice split the night. "He's here."

Sandra looked across the road. David Sullivan was walking straight towards them.

*

Sullivan had paused in the door-well of Black's, waited until he was sure it was safe then began to cross the road. He slipped the shotgun back into his inside pocket and found the keys to his bike: a Harley Electra-Glide in midnight blue. He stopped admired it for a second. Had always wanted one. Why not now?

Straddling the seat he took the helmet from the handlebars. About to place it on his head, he saw two figures step from behind the car on his left. Hoods concealed their faces but Sullivan wasn't looking, he was focused on the cheap Russian automatic one of them had in his hand. He held it sideways like he had seen in the movies.

"Go 'ead, lad. Do it." The other spoke, urging him to fire while he strutted in front of Sullivan. "This is what you get when you fuck with us," he said and elbowed his friend with the gun. "Go on Chris. Prove you've got the bottle."

"No." The shout echoed and Sullivan saw Sandra running from the shadows. She was sobbing. "Don't, Chris, don't do it." She tried to grab him but he flung back the hand holding the gun. It caught her face and a gash appeared. Blood flowed and she fell back, clutched her cheek.

Sullivan hadn't moved. The boy's hood had fallen from his head and lay on his shoulder. He stared at him, had seen him before. And as he stared down the barrel of the gun and the boy named Chris tightened his finger on the trigger, had to admit that yeah, there really was something about the kid that reminded him of himself.

The Big Shot

Aidan cursed. The shower was hot, soothing, part of his routine. Didn't appreciate the phone ringing in the middle of it. Still he answered, thought it best to show some willing. Seemed a kid had been hit, one in the leg and one in the head as he lay in the road screaming for his mother. Nobody was going to miss him, obnoxious shit that he was, but he was one of theirs, one of Eric's crew. And Aidan had his orders – "Get it sorted."

The kick of adrenaline cleared his mind. Felt sharper than he had in years. Two years in Spain was enough to dull anyone's senses. Thought he'd be there forever. But family ties, loyalty and the lure of home dragged him back. So he lived with regrets and the doubts of his trade; that maybe he was past it, that maybe he was losing his edge. He turned, checked his profile in the mirror. Doubts receded. Aidan had a physique better than a man half his age. Satisfied, he strolled into his little brother's room.

Danny was a lump beneath the covers. He rattled the bed. "Get up and phone your brother. Tell Neal we need some wheels." Danny didn't move. Aidan didn't ask twice. He pushed his hands beneath the mattress and lifted. Boy, bedclothes and mattress fell to the floor. "C'mon lazy arse." But the only movement was a pale arm snaking from the sheets and reaching for a pillow. Aidan shook his head, called Neal himself.

He was in the kitchen drinking tea with Neal when Danny finally emerged from his room. He shuffled to the kettle. Aidan frowned. His kid brother had a sickly, grey pallor. "You wanna lay off the booze kid. You look like death." His face hardened. "Hey, you better not be getting into any weird shit. Start sticking stuff up your nose and you're out."

"Fuck off Aidan. You're not my keeper."

"No?"

"No. You're just an ugly cunt who likes throwing his weight around."

"Touchy aren't yer?"

"It's what you get chasing women." Neal's smirk lit the room. He stubbed his cigarette into the ashtray and pushed a strand of black hair behind his ear.

Aidan perked up. "Women? What sort of women?"

"The wrong sort. Little blonde tart."

Danny snarled. "She's not a tart."

Neal's smug demeanour evaporated. He lifted a finger, began to poke the air, but before a word left his mouth, Aidan banged the table. "Enough."

Danny glowered, dared Neal to continue, but Neal knew better than to defy his elder brother and held his hands up submissively. Drama over. In the corner the kettle began to rattle. "And put water in that thing," said Aidan, "before you blow the friggin' element." The fire in Danny's eyes died. Reluctantly, he obeyed.

Aidan took a breath, wafted Neal's cigarette smoke back across the table. "So," he said. "Whaddya get?"

"Merc – AMG."

"Fuck me." Aidan ran a palm across the crown of his head, stared across the table. "Ever hear the word discreet, Nee? It means obscure, unobtrusive?"

Neal shrugged, "Good car. Fast, like."

"Don't care how fast it is, just so no one clocks us."

Neal's gypsy eyes glinted. "It's a Merc," he said, and smiled. "Who cares?"

"Jesus." Aidan shook his head. Following his Spanish exile, he had brought his brothers into Eric's fold. Danny was still a prospect and Neal – well he wondered if Neal would ever take the job seriously. He gestured him closer, "Lose the Merc." He jabbed a thumb in Danny's direction, "Take him and find another." He lowered his voice. "And Nee – a Vectra or Mondeo will do."

*

An hour later they were back. Aidan was in the living room listening to Jazz FM on the radio. He lowered the sound and "Goodbye, Porkpie Hat" faded away. "Well?"

Neal's nose twitched in distaste. "P-reg Astra – nice family saloon."

"Good," he said and rose from the armchair. Taking his leather jacket from behind the door he felt the pockets. Aidan watched Danny's face, saw his interest as he withdrew the hammerless Iver Johnson and checked the chamber. The piece was almost an antique, but the silver revolver was a favourite. "Wanna hold it?" Danny shook his head. Aidan grimaced. Sooner or later he would have to harden the kid up.

"Where to?" Neal held the door open.

"Let's see Stan. If anyone knows, he will."

*

Eric ran Liverpool's south end. It was his patch, his domain. On the western fringe, amidst the new developments and overlooking the river, was an old favourite of Aidan's. The Bridge was out of the way and would never make it onto a tourist's itinerary. But it had its uses. Many a dispute was settled over a quiet pint in the back room and the car park was plenty big enough for a "straightener" to settle the score. Stan's ice cream van sat across the road.

Aidan wound down the side window. "How's biz, Stan?"

Stan's fleshy face peered over the counter. His idle demeanour did nothing to disguise quick, anxious eyes. "Usual."

Aidan nodded. "And the ciggies?"

Stan smiled sheepishly. November was a lean time for ice cream, but with a thriving side line in contraband tobacco, he was never going to starve. His face twitched. "Same."

Aidan pursed his lips. "Give us a couple of wafers. He glanced behind. "And a

Ninety-nine for our kid." He watched Danny's face darken, but was glad to see the boy knew when to keep his mouth shut.

Like a white-coated mole, Stan dug down into the fridge. "Hear about the shooting?"

"Bad business," said Aidan. He took a wafer from one of Stan's paddle-like hands, passed another to Neal.

Stan shook his head. "Place is going from bad to worse."

Aidan licked the bottom edge. "Whaddya know?"

"Only what I hear."

"Which is?"

Stan wrinkled his face, twirled a cone beneath, Mr Whippy – Ice Cream Maker.

"South End Boys."

"Who?"

"South End Boys," he repeated, sticking a flake in the

pyramid of ice. "Bunch of little fuckers. It was them done the post office couple of weeks back. Stuck a gun in the old girl's face and rode off on bikes." Cone in one hand, red syrup in the other, he looked through the window at Danny. Deliberately he cautioned himself. "Or... that's what people say." Stan squeezed the bottle.

Aidan's face was blank. "People? What people? And who the hell are these

South End Boys?"

"Kids, Aidan, that's all, just kids." He leant out of the hatch, passed the ice cream down.

"And they get away with it?"

"You've been gone a long time," said Stan, "things change."

Aidan stroked his chin, eyed Stan, knew the shyster of old. He may act the fool but knew the score. And he had a big mouth. "Want names, Stan. Who done it?"

Stan lowered his voice. "Look," he said. "I keep me head down, nobody has trouble from me, you know that. I keep out of their way. Especially after what happened to Frankie."

Aidan rolled his eyes. "And what happened to Frankie?"

"Hit him with a crowbar, Aidan. Hit him and gave him a bloody good hiding.

Poor bastard's only just come out of hozzie."

Aidan grimaced. "You're not helping, Stan."

Stan blinked, knew there would be no peace until he said something. "There is one thing," he said. "The kid who was shot," he looked furtively around, "was one of the gang."

"One of these South End lot. But he worked for Eric?"

"Things go on, Aidan."

"Not here they don't. Why was he shot?"

"Look, they all want to be The Big I Am, a Big Shot, King Dick for a day. If it means ripping Eric off, then so be it. Kid was doing a bit of freelance work. Sold hash to the kids."

"Little bastard. If he wasn't dead, I'd kill him."

"Probably fell out with the capo. Not getting his cut or something."

"And who's that?"

Stan barked a laugh. "Million dollar question, Aidan. No one knows. Kid keeps a low profile. All of 'em do. And if they're out on the street, hoods pulled up, scarves round faces," he shook his head. "Can't tell one from the other. No, Aidan. You won't find anyone who knows."

Aidan let it pass, would do another time. But he still had work to do. He narrowed his eyes. "Still want a name though."

"Don't know any names."

"Think you do Stan," Aidan's voice was flat, cold, controlled. "Who pulled the trigger?"

Stan began to shake. "I've said too much. These kids got no fear." His voice quivered. "If they knew it was me..."

"Listen you bag of shit, you tell me what I want to know or it won't be the kids you have to worry about." Aidan made a show of putting his hand in his pocket where a fist-sized bulge revealed the revolver's shape.

Stan's face drained of colour. This time he didn't hesitate. "There were two.

Didn't see 'em Aidan, believe me I didn't. But a name's been mentioned."

"Well?"

There was no going back so Stan just told him. "John McCreedy."

"McCreedy?"

Stan nodded.

Satisfied, Aidan took his hand out of his pocket. "And where might I find Mr

John McCreedy?"

Stan's shoulders hunched and he shook his head. "Don't know that, Aidan."

Aidan moved his hand a fraction closer to his pocket.

Stan sighed, bowed to the inevitable. "Right now, he'll be in Millie's getting pissed."

"Hope you're right Stan."

"I do my best, you know I do."

But Aidan was no longer listening. Neal had started the car and as they were pulling away, Stan's final words flew through the open window. "Hey, tell Eric I was asking after him."

*

Millie's was a rundown, scruffy, anonymous bar in a part of town that needed another rundown, scruffy, anonymous bar like a hole in the head. Once it had been vibrant, bounced to live bands, or rocked to a DJ's discs. Now it was a sad reminder of days gone by, only frequented by those who needed the comfort of the familiar, an escape from life, or had nowhere else to go. In the adjacent parking bay, a P-reg Astra with three occupants watched the door.

"What do we know about McCreedy?" Aidan looked at the decrepit building, shook his head. Wondered what had happened to the place.

For a moment neither brother spoke. Then Neal twisted his neck, looked at Danny in the back. "Didn't you go to school with him?"

Danny squirmed. "We were in the same year."

"What's he like?" Aidan was curious.

"Okay."

"Just okay?"

"Yeah."

Aidan sighed. Wasn't going to get much help there. Was about to thank him for his contribution when Danny thrust his head forward.

"He was all right y'know. Quiet, like." He shook his head. "Can't believe he's involved. Maybe Stan's got it wrong."

"It's a name," said Aidan. "Besides, it don't really matter. It's a gesture is all. A message to others that Eric's still got his eye on the ball." He cracked his knuckles. "So you'd recognise McCreedy?"

"Sure."

"Good." Aidan took a deep breath. "You're with me." He opened the door and with Danny beside him, walked towards the pub. "If he's there, give me the nod."

Inside, Millie's had all the ambience of a tomb without the finesse. Aidan's nose twitched. Stale tobacco, old men's sweat, and spillage from a thousand and one beers combined to create one unwholesome musk. Waiting while his eyes adjusted to the watery light, he looked around the sparsely populated room. Mismatched tables and chairs, threadbare carpet, and red vinyl seats repaired with gaffa tape reminded him of Saturday night at the A&E. The wooden bar was rough, sharp edged; the men around it the same. Some moved away when they saw Aidan, knew him from old. Finished their drinks elsewhere. Aidan paid no heed. Taking a Bud for the boy and a JD for himself, he pushed Danny into an empty seat, scanned the room with a predatory eye.

"Is he here?"

Danny shook his head. Aidan grimaced, disappointed. He thought, hoped, the affair could be wrapped up in an afternoon. Now it looked like it would drag on, searching for the little twat until he could mete out his brand of justice. He turned to his drink, had barely touched it when he saw the girl. Pretty but cheap, she was coming out of the Ladies, brushing away a blonde fringe that had fallen over one eye. She made her way to a table littered with empty bottles where a boy with bleached hair and a tattoo of a bird on the left side of his neck sat rolling a cigarette. She kissed him, grabbed a bottle, drank from its open top.

Danny jerked back in his seat, started to rise. Aidan touched his arm. "Easy, lad.

That him?" Danny nodded. Aidan glanced behind. Beer on the table, hand up her skirt, John McCreedy looked like he was having a good day. Let him have his day, thought Aidan, because a day was all he was going to get. He motioned to Danny, who didn't move. "Dan." He punched him on the arm. "C'mon." He jutted his chin towards the door. They slipped from the room.

Outside Aidan caught Danny's sleeve. "You okay?"

"Sure."

"Getting windy?"

"No."

Aidan laid a hand on the boy's shoulder, tried to imbue him with a sense of his own strength. "You could take him on your own."

Danny's face was blank. He turned towards the car and thrust his hands deep into his pockets. "I know."

Aidan stopped, watched his brother, watched him climb inside the car. Danny and Neal. He shook his head. One day he wouldn't be there. One day they would have to stand on their own, look after each other, learn how to put it on the line and not take a step back. Aidan pursed his lips. One way or another, he would make sure they did.

*

Night had come. It was cold and damp in the Astra and the three men watching the door of Millie's shuffled inside their jackets. Just for a moment Aidan allowed his eyes to stray. He glanced at Danny. The boy was growing impatient.

"When?"

Aidan's face was impassive. "When I say." He turned, refocused on the building, waited for the serious part of the day to begin.

On his lap was a black revolver. An hour earlier he had set the boys to watch and gone back to the house. Knew exactly where to go, had put it beneath the floorboards of the family home years before. It was a deactivated Webley once owned by a geek who played soldiers at weekends. Impossible to trace. A friend had bored out the barrel. Inaccurate at anything over ten feet, he once told Danny. "If you're that far away, you're not doing your job." Cleaned and oiled, like him, it was ready to go.

The hours moved slowly. Neal smoked, Aidan's barbed comments drew no response until he opened the window and let an icy blast fill the car. The smoking stopped. A squall blew in from the river. The tarmac glistened, the houses were still. And then it happened.

Aidan let out a low breath. "Now." He was out of the car and marching towards Millie's before Neal and Danny even realised he had gone.

Danny hurried to catch him.

Aidan had seen McCreedy's shadow in the opening. A moment later his body materialised. He held an arm against the door frame, steadying himself, unsure whether to vomit or fall. It passed and he grabbed the girl around the waist, whispered in her ear. They were laughing. Too late he saw Aidan.

"Wha..."

Aidan grabbed the back of his neck, tore him away from the girl, slammed his face into the door frame. There was a crack of cartilage and gristle as his nose turned to mush. He fell to his knees. Aidan was ready and dragged him into the alley alongside.

The girl hadn't moved. Fear froze her to the spot. She saw Danny, sobered quickly. He grabbed her arm, tugged, tugged so hard it hurt, and pulled her into the alley behind McCreedy. She started to plead, but a shake of his head was enough. "Shut it," he said, "shut it now."

Good. The boy had heart, thought Aidan, and he kicked McCreedy in the guts. He turned to the girl. "Fuck off kid. Fuck off and don't come back."

"But you can't…"

Aidan caught her with the back of his hand. "I said go home."

She held her cheek, the shock seeping through her defiance like the tears trickling through her mascara. She looked at him. His eyes were as cold and hard as gun-metal and she knew there was nothing here but the promise of pain. She darted a glance at Danny, swallowed, began to back away. Out of the alley she hesitated, looked once then turned and ran. She didn't look back.

Aidan grunted, waited till the click clack of her heels faded to nothing and switched his attention to McCreedy. Blood was flowing from his nose. Aidan sneered. That was the least of his problems. He took the silver revolver from his pocket. Made sure McCreedy saw it. "Got the tape?" he said and Danny held up a black roll, tore a piece off and fastened it over McCreedy's mouth. "Hands." McCreedy made no sense of the word but a cuff with the pistol to the back of his head improved his hearing. "Hands." This time he bent forward, meekly placing them behind him while Danny wound tape around his wrists.

The Astra waited at the alley's entrance, doors open. Trussed like a hog, McCreedy was dragged and pushed into the back seat. Gun in his ribs, Aidan sat beside him while Danny climbed into the passenger seat. Tyres screeched as they raced away.

*

They headed out of town, swift and fast until Neal detoured off the tarmac and followed what was little more than a dirt track onto waste ground. He slowed then stopped. Ahead was the promenade, the river, and a derelict landing stage where festival goers had once disgorged to see the famous gardens. Long time ago. The gardens were as derelict as the landing stage. On the far side a tanker disgorged its cargo. Lights blazed, men worked, but here it was quiet. Nothing to disturb these men at work. Aidan shoved McCreedy out of the car, pushed him onto the rotten timbers of the landing stage.

McCreedy slipped, knew there was nothing between him and

the darkness. Below, he could hear water lapping against the wooden pontoons. Aidan forced him to his knees.

"One chance kid," he held a finger in front of his eyes, "that's all you get," and he pulled the tape from his mouth.

McCreedy tasted the air, gasped. "Why – why are you doing this?" he said.

Aidan walked to the end of the landing stage, looked over the edge. "Who pulled the trigger?"

"What?"

Aidan sauntered back. "You or your mate?"

McCreedy looked up, saw Aidan's face and knew he was in shit up to his neck. Ten paces away he saw Danny and bit his lip. "Don't know what you mean."

Aidan's voice hardened, but still he remained reasonable. So he gave the boy his chance. "You were seen. We know there were two. If it was the other who did the shooting you'll just get a hiding. Nothing else, I promise." He walked to Danny, passed him the revolver. "If not," and he pulled the Webley from his waistband. The implication was clear. This was his killing gun.

McCreedy stopped breathing, gasped. "Not me."

"Then who, shit-for-brains? I want a name."

McCreedy's world was crashing around him. In ten minutes he'd gone from King

Dick to a quivering mass of puke and blood. He stared into the abyss. "Danny." He squeezed the name through gritted teeth.

Aidan slapped him. "School pal or not, you'll get no help there. This is between you and me."

But behind him, Danny had stepped onto the patchwork timbers. "Tell him, Creedy," he said. "Tell him everything. Tell him about the boys and the way it works. Tell him about loyalty."

McCreedy saw the silver pistol in Danny's hand. Just for a moment it seemed a door had opened. He looked into Aidan's face. Hope made him a fool. He laughed. "You can't touch me," he said. "Hurt one, you hurt us all." He jutted his jaw, stared at Aidan. "You do, they'll tear you apart."

Aidan roared. His scream ripped the night. He cracked the pistol against McCreedy's head. "You're a maggot, a fucking maggot. This is my patch, my territory, tread on it you tread on me. Nothing else counts boy – just this," and he pushed the gun beneath McCreedy's nose. "Now tell me what I want to know.

Who killed him?"

Sprawled on the decking, blood pulsing from the cut on his head, he pushed himself away from Aidan knowing there was nowhere to hide. Clambering to his knees, he saw Aidan's gun an inch from his eyes. The bird tattoo on his neck pulsed. "Not me," he hissed. "I told you," and he turned his eyes on Danny. "Him!"

Aidan stepped back, wasn't sure what he'd heard. Was about to whip him again, but a single shot came from the dark and John McCreedy's head flew back. He rocked forward, his dead eyes on the boy he called friend – then he tumbled backwards, down into the black water of the Mersey. Aidan heard the splash, stared after him. Saw nothing but the river. All that was left of John McCreedy was a dark patch of blood that would be washed away by the rain. He stared at Danny. "Why?"

"Shouldn't have been with my girl."

"Your girl?" Aidan frowned, glanced at Neal leaning on the bonnet of the car. "The little blonde tart?" Neal smirked, nodded. Aidan's confusion was beginning to clear. "And last night?"

"Kid crossed me. Like Stan said, I take my cut."

Aidan let out a half-hearted laugh. "So you run the South End Boys. Suppose I should have guessed." He looked at Danny with grudging respect. "So we're not so different after all."

Danny snorted. "You having a laugh? I work for me. You're owned by a dickhead."

Aidan's shoulders swept back. "You watch your mouth kid, if Eric finds out…"

"I don't give a flying fuck about Eric." He looked at Aidan. "Eric and those around him are finished. This is my town."

Aidan closed his eyes, had heard it a thousand times before. "So you want to be a

Big Shot. If it wasn't for us being family…"

"Family." Danny snarled. "When I was ten the house got repossessed. Me, Neal and Mam had nowhere to go. You were on remand in Walton. And where were you when she died?" He sneered, "Fucking Spain." He stared at his elder brother. "You should have stayed there."

Aidan's anger rose like a black tide. He twisted his head, looked at Neal. "You in this as well?"

Neal shrugged. "Keeping my options open. Besides," he said and his smirk was the final straw, "I'd rather have a Merc than an

Astra."

"Lousy bastard." Aidan switched focus, quickly brought the Webley to bear on Danny and fired. Fifteen paces away, the bullet whistled harmlessly over Danny's head. The ghost of a smile spread across his kid brother's face. Slowly, like a latter day duellist, Danny raised the silver pistol. He cocked his head to one side and sneered.

"Don't believe you're doing your job properly," he said. And pulled the trigger twice.

If you enjoyed *Breaking Even*, why not try our other Armley Press titles available from Amazon and through UK bookshops?

Mick McCann
Coming Out as a Bowie Fan
ISBN 0-9554699-0-2

Mick McCann
Nailed
ISBN 0-9554699-2-9

Mick McCann
How Leeds Changed the World
ISBN 0-9554699-3-0

John Lake
Hot Knife
ISBN 0-9554699-1-6

John Lake
Blowback
ISBN 0-9554699-4-7

John Lake
Speedbomb
ISBN 0-9554699-5-4

John Lake
Amy and the Fox
ISBN 0-9934811-0-9

Ray Brown
In All Beginnings
ISBN 0-9554699-6-1

Samantha Priestley
Reliability of Rope
ISBN 0-9554699-8-5

Chris Nickson
Leeds, the Biography
ISBN 0-9554699-7-8

Nathan O'Hagan
The World is (Not) a Cold Dead Place
ISBN 0-9554699-9-2

Visit *armleypress.com*

www.ingramcontent.com/pod-product-compliance
Lightning Source LLC
Chambersburg PA
CBHW020910180626
46816CB00007BA/2333